Dear Harlequin Desire R

We are thrilled to welcome back a very op
book this month: *A Contract Engagement* by #1 *New York Times* and *USA TODAY* bestselling author Maya Banks, originally published as *Billionaire's Contract Engagement*. This classic Harlequin Desire novel, part of the Kings of the Boardroom series, delivers everything you want—glamour, drama, loads of sensual tension and the sexiest of alpha heroes—from one of your favorite authors.

Returning this novel to our publishing lineup is a tribute to our loyal readers and a testament to the endurance of your choice for entertaining reading. Stories that feature a world of connected characters and intense, passionate drama have long prevailed as your preferred brand of exceptional contemporary romance at Harlequin Desire. The story of billionaire businessman Evan Reese is no exception. He's wanted Celia Taylor for six months, and he finally has an opportunity to make her his—at least temporarily. He'll sign the deal she wants, but only if she plays the role of his fake fiancée at a family wedding!

Because we know you can't resist a CEO intent on seduction—or a happy ending—we hope you enjoy this enduring fan favorite.

Happy reading!

Stacy Boyd

Senior Editor

A CONTRACT ENGAGEMENT

—

MAYA BANKS

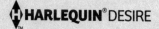
HARLEQUIN® DESIRE

Special thanks and acknowledgment to Maya Banks for her contribution to The Kings of the Boardroom series.

ISBN-13: 978-0-373-73414-6

A Contract Engagement

Recycling programs for this product may not exist in your area.

Printed in U.S.A.

www.Harlequin.com

Maya Banks has loved romance novels from a very (very) early age, and almost from the start she dreamed of writing them, as well. In her teens she filled countless notebooks with overdramatic stories of love and passion. Today her stories are only slightly less dramatic, but no less romantic.

She lives in Texas with her husband and three children and wouldn't contemplate living anywhere other than the South. When she's not writing, she's usually hunting, fishing or playing poker. She loves to hear from readers, and she can be found online at mayabanks.com, or you can email her at maya@mayabanks.com.

Books by Maya Banks

Visit the Author Profile page
at Harlequin.com, or mayabanks.com,
for more titles.

To Elizabeth Edwards—thank you so much for allowing me to pick your brain. The information was invaluable and helped me to really wrap my mind around these characters.

And for Diana—you'll be missed!

One

The vultures were circling.

Celia Taylor stood back, wineglass in hand, and surveyed the crowded ballroom. The fund-raiser was supposed to be more pleasure than business, but business was uppermost on the minds of her competition.

Across the room, Evan Reese stood in a large group of people. He looked relaxed, seemingly in his element, an easy smile making his extraordinarily handsome face even more gorgeous.

It should be a crime for a man to be that good-looking. Tall, rugged, he looked every inch the kind of man who'd be at home in the athletic wear his company designed and sold. There was an aura of confidence and power around him, and above all, Celia loved a man who was sure of himself.

Given the long, searching glances they'd exchanged over the last few weeks, she'd be a fool not to entertain the idea of seeing where things could lead.

If he wasn't a prospective client.

A client she wanted to land very much.

She wanted the account—her boss and the agency was counting on her—but she drew the line at sleeping with a man to get what she wanted.

Celia turned away from the sight of Evan Reese before she became too enthralled in just watching him. They'd performed a delicate dance around each other ever since he'd fired his last advertising agency. He knew she wanted him—in the professional sense of course. Hell, he probably knew she wanted him naked and in bed too, but she wasn't going to dwell on that. Maybe later tonight when she could afford to indulge in a little fantasy.

The problem was, anytime a big company like Reese Enterprises fired an agency, it became open season. The other agencies circled like sharks. It was a dog-eat-dog world, and in reality, she should be over there, shoving herself down his throat like the rest of her competition, but she couldn't help but believe Evan Reese was secretly amused by the attention. He took a different hand. She was sure of it.

"Celia, glad you made it. Have you spoken to Reese yet?"

Celia turned to see her boss, Brock Maddox, standing a foot away. He wasn't drinking. He didn't even look particularly thrilled to be here.

Her eyebrow rose. "A tux. Why, Brock, you look positively decadent. However are you keeping the ladies at bay?"

He grunted in response, his lips curling in distaste. "Cut it out, Celia. I brought Elle along."

Celia looked beyond his shoulder to see his pretty assistant standing a few feet away. When Elle looked her way, Celia smiled and waved.

"You look beautiful," Celia mouthed.

Elle smiled and ducked her head self-consciously but not before Celia saw the faint blush that colored her cheeks.

Brock gestured impatiently toward Evan. "Why are you standing over here while Evan Reese is over there?" Brock scanned the room and his expression hardened. "I should have known the old bastard would be here."

Celia followed his gaze to see Athos Koteas holding court within hearing distance of Evan. Though she wouldn't admit it to Brock, it made her extremely nervous to see their business rival hammering so relentlessly on Evan Reese. Koteas owned Golden Gate Promotions, and not only had Koteas lured away a few of Maddox's top clients in recent months, he'd also launched a PR campaign against Maddox. It was dirty pool, but it in no way surprised Celia. Koteas was ruthless, and he'd do anything to win.

"Well, yes," Celia murmured. "His ad execs are busy working Evan over."

"Any reason you aren't?"

She laid her hand on his forearm. She knew how important this account was to Brock—to everyone at Maddox Communications. "I need you to trust me, Brock. I've studied Evan Reese extensively. He knows I'm interested. He'll come to me eventually. I'm sure of it."

"Are you fifty million dollars sure, Celia? Maddox is small, and this kind of deal means our employees keep their jobs whereas if we continue to lose clients and accounts, I can't make any guarantees."

"I know I'm asking a lot," she said in a low voice. "But I can't walk over there and pull out the seductive wiles." She gestured toward the women standing around Evan. They weren't making any bones as to how far they'd go to sign him. "It's what he expects, and you of all people know I can't do it. I can land this account on the *ideas,* Brock. I've spent every waking minute putting this pitch together. There's no way he won't go for it."

Brock studied her for a long moment, his eyes gleaming with what looked like respect. She loved working for him. He was hard. He was demanding. And he was the only person she'd presented her side of what had happened in New York in her last advertising job.

"I never expected you to land the account on anything less than your brilliance, Celia," Brock said softly. "I hope I never gave you any other impression."

"I know. I appreciate your confidence more than you know. I won't let you down. I won't let Maddox Communications down."

Brock ran a hand through his hair and glanced once more across the room. He looked tired. It was true he worked hard. The agency was everything to him. But in the last few months new lines had appeared around his eyes. More than anything Celia wanted to be able to hand this account to him. He had believed in her when everyone else was willing to think the worst.

She glanced up to see Evan threading his way through the throng of people. "Don't look now, but he's headed our way. Maybe you should take Elle and go dance or something."

As quickly as he'd approached, Brock turned and melted back into the crowd.

Celia sipped at her wine and practiced nonchalance as she literally felt Evan close in. It was impossible to miss him. Her body always seemed to heat up about five degrees whenever he was anywhere near.

And his smell. Even amid the hustle and bustle of the crowded room, the mix of so many feminine perfumes, she could pick out his unique scent. Rough. Masculine and mouthwateringly sexy. It made no sense to her, but she was attuned to his every nuance, and that had nothing to do with all the studying up she'd done on him and his company.

"Celia," he murmured.

She turned with a welcoming smile. "Hello, Evan. Enjoying the evening?"

"I think you know I'm not."

She raised one eyebrow and stared at him over the rim of her glass. "Do I?"

Evan snagged a flute from a passing waiter and turned his attention fully on her. It was all she could do not to gasp under his heated scrutiny. It was as if he undressed her right then and there in front of a roomful of people. Her blood simmered and pooled low in her belly. He had beautiful eyes, and they were currently devouring her, delving beneath the modest evening gown she'd chosen. He made it seem like she wore the most scanty, revealing dress imaginable. She felt nude and vulnerable under his searing gaze.

"Tell me something, Celia. Why aren't you over with the rest of the piranhas convincing me that your ad agency will take Reese Enterprises straight to the top?"

Her lips curved upward into a smile. "Because you already are at the top?"

"You're such a tease."

At that her smile faded. He was right. She was flirting, and it was the last thing she wanted to do.

She glanced across the room to where the other ad execs stood staring holes through her and Evan.

"I'm not desperate, Evan. I know I'm good. I know my ideas for your ad campaign are spectacular. Does that make me arrogant? Maybe. But I don't need to sell you on a load of malarkey. All I need is the time to show you what Maddox Communications can do for you."

"What *you* can do for me, Celia."

Her eyes widened in surprise at the blatant innuendo. And then he went on to correct the errant assumption she'd just made.

"If the ideas are yours and are as brilliant as you say, I'd hardly be taking on Maddox and what the agency could do for me. I'd be hiring you."

She frowned and hated that she suddenly felt at a disadvantage. Her fingers curled a little tighter around the glass, and she prayed they wouldn't shake and betray her unease.

He studied her curiously, having obviously picked up on her discomfort.

"It wasn't a proposition, Celia. Believe me, you'd know the difference."

In a daring move, he reached a finger out and traced a line down the bare skin of her arm. She was unable to call back the shiver, or the sprinkling of chill bumps that danced over her flesh.

"I only meant that if you wow me with a pitch and I sign on with Maddox, you won't pawn me off to some junior executive. I'd expect you to oversee the campaign at every level."

"And do you anticipate signing with Maddox Communications?" she asked huskily.

There was a gleam of amusement in his green eyes. He took a measured sip of his wine and then regarded her lazily. "If your pitch is good enough. Golden Gate has some good ideas. I'm considering them."

Her lips tightened. "Only because you haven't seen mine yet."

He smiled again. "I like confidence. I don't like false modesty. I look forward to seeing what you have in mind, Celia Taylor. I have a feeling you put every bit of that passion I see burning in your eyes into your work. Brock Maddox is a lucky man to have such a fierce employee. I wonder if he knows it."

"Are we moving into the appointment phase?" she asked lightly. "I have to admit, I've enjoyed watching you surrounded by the piranhas as you call them."

He put his glass down on a nearby table. "Dance with me and we'll discuss appointment times."

Her eyes narrowed.

He lifted one finely constructed eyebrow into what looked like a challenge.

"I've also danced with female ad executives from Golden Gate, Primrose, San Fran Media—"

She held up her hand. "Okay, okay, I get it. You're making your selection on who's the best dance partner."

He threw back his head and laughed. Several people around them turned to stare, and she had to resist the strong urge to flee the room. She hated the attention that Evan seemed to have no issue with whatsoever. How nice it must be not to have to worry what people thought about you. To have your reputation intact and not have suffered the stupidity and vindictiveness of others. But then men rarely suffered in cases like hers. It was always the woman. The vilified other woman.

Knowing no graceful way to bow out of the dance, she set down her own glass and allowed Evan to lead her onto the ballroom floor.

To her relief, he held her loosely. To anyone looking on, they could find no fault or impropriety. She and Evan didn't look like lovers, but she knew the thought was present in both their minds. She could see the desire in his eyes and knew he could probably see it in hers.

She wasn't practiced at hiding her emotions. Maybe being the only girl in an all-male household growing up was the reason. Her family was a loud, demonstrative lot, and she'd always been regarded as the precious daughter and sister.

It would make her life easier to be able to hide her thoughts from this man. Then she wouldn't concern herself over whether he was giving her a shot because he thought she deserved it or whether he was thinking only of the powerful sexual pull between them and how best to capitalize on it.

Wow, Celia. Lump him in with all the other jerks you've known, why don't you? Nothing like being tried and convicted based on your gender.

"Relax. You're thinking way too much," Evan murmured close to her ear.

She forced herself to do as he'd instructed and gave herself over to the beautiful music and the sheer enjoyment of dancing with a man who took her breath away.

"So how is next week? I have Friday free."

She jerked back to reality, and for a moment couldn't for the life of her figure out what he was talking about. Some professional she was.

"I was thinking we could meet informally and you could go over what you have in mind. If I'm interested we could do the whole shebang at your agency. Maybe that'll save us both a lot of time and hassle if I'm not loving your ideas."

"Sure. I can do Friday. Friday is good."

The music ended, and he held her just a bit longer than necessary, but she was so affected by the intensity of his gaze that she couldn't formulate a single objection.

"I'll have my assistant call you with the time and location then."

He picked up her hand and brought it to his lips. The warm brush of his mouth over the back of her hand sent a bolt of pleasure straight down her spine.

"Until Friday."

She watched wordlessly as he strolled away. He was immediately swallowed up by a crowd of people again, but he turned and found her gaze. For a moment they simply stared at one another and then the corners of his mouth lifted into a half smile.

Oh, yes, he knew. He knew exactly what her reaction to him was. He'd have to be a complete moron not to. And he was anything but. The man was smart. He was driven. And he had a reputation for being ruthless. He was the perfect client.

She turned to walk toward the exit. She'd done what she'd come for. There was no reason to stick around and be social. If there was any gossip over her dance with Evan, she certainly didn't want to hear it.

On the way, she passed Brock and Elle, who were standing somewhat awkwardly to the side. Brock didn't say anything. He just lifted an inquiring brow. Of course he would have seen her dancing with Evan. Brock probably hadn't looked at anyone but Evan all night. A shame, really, since Elle looked fabulous in her black sheath.

"Friday," she said in a low voice. "I meet with him Friday. No formal pitch. He wants to hear my ideas first. If he likes them, he'll arrange a time for us to hit him with both barrels."

Brock nodded, and she saw the gleam of satisfaction light his eyes.

"Good work, Celia."

Celia smiled and resumed her path to the door. She had a lot to do before next Friday.

Evan Reese loosened his tie as soon as he walked into his hotel suite. He left a trail of clothing from the door, where he threw his jacket over one of the chairs, to the bedroom where he peeled off his socks and left them on the floor.

The desk with his laptop and briefcase beckoned, but for once, the idea of work didn't appeal to him. He was too preoccupied with thoughts of Celia Taylor.

Beautiful, seductive, impossibly aloof Celia Taylor.

His body had been on heightened sense of alert ever since she walked into the ballroom, and though he'd known the moment she left, he was still tense and painfully aware of her scent, how she felt in his arms, how her skin felt under his fingers the one time he'd been bold enough to touch her.

He wanted to do a hell of a lot more than just touch. He wanted to taste her. He wanted her underneath him, making all those feminine, breathy sounds of a woman being pleasured.

He wanted to slide his hand between those gorgeous legs and spread her thighs. He would spend all night making love to her. A woman such as Celia wasn't to be rushed. No, he'd get to know every inch of her body. Find out where she liked to be touched and kissed.

His fixation with her couldn't be readily explained. It wasn't as though he lived as a monk. He had sex. He never lacked for partners. Sex was good. But he knew that sex with Celia would never be just good. It would be lush and delicious. The kind of experience a man would sell his soul for.

She was indeed a beautiful woman. Tall, but not too tall. She would fit perfectly against him, her head tucked just underneath his chin. She often wore her long red hair up in a loose style that told him she didn't pay a lot of attention to whether every strand was in place.

He wanted to take that damn clip out, toss it in the garbage and watch as her silken mass spilled down her back. Or better yet, let it spill over him while they made love.

He cursed under his breath when his body reacted to that image. Cold showers didn't do a thing for his hunger. He ought to know. He'd taken enough of them over the last few weeks.

Perhaps her most mesmerizing feature was her eyes. An unusual shade of green. At times they looked more blue but in certain lighting they were vivid green.

The more cynical side of him wondered why a woman that beautiful hadn't tried to seduce him into hiring her agency. It wasn't like it hadn't been attempted before. In fact, he'd received two such propositions tonight at the fund-raiser.

He wasn't saying he'd mind. Right now he'd use just about any reason to get into Celia Taylor's bed. But there was a reserve about her that intrigued him. She was a cool customer, and he admired that. She wanted the account. She'd made no bones about that. But she hadn't actively pursued him.

No, she'd waited for him to come to her, and maybe that made her damn smart since he'd done just that.

The ring of his BlackBerry disturbed his fantasy and brought him sharply back to the present. He looked down in disgust at the unmistakable ridge in his trousers then reached into his pocket for his phone.

His mother. He frowned. He wasn't really in the mood for anything to do with his family, but he loved his mother dearly, and he couldn't very well ignore her.

With a resigned sigh, he punched the answer button and put the phone to his ear.

"Hello, Mom."

"Evan! I'm so glad I caught you. You're so busy these days."

He could hear the disapproval and worry in her voice.

"The business doesn't run itself," he reminded her.

She made a low sound of exasperation. "You sound so much like your father."

He winced. That wasn't exactly at the top of the list of things he wanted to hear.

"I wanted to call to make sure you hadn't forgotten about this weekend. It's important to Mitchell that you be there."

There was a note of anxiety in her voice that always seemed to creep in when his brother was mentioned.

"You can't think I'd actually go to their wedding," Evan said mildly. And the only important thing to Mitchell was that Evan be there to see his triumph.

His mother made a disapproving sound. "I know it won't be easy for you, Evan. But don't you think you should for- give him? It's obvious he and Bettina belong together. It would be so nice to have the whole family back together again."

"Easy? It won't be easy *or* difficult, Mom. I don't care, and frankly they're welcome to each other. I simply don't have the time or the desire to attend."

"Would you do it for me?" she begged. "Please. I want just one time to see my sons in the same room."

Evan sank onto the edge of the bed and pinched the bridge of his nose between two fingers. If his dad had called, he would have had no problem refusing. If Mitchell had called, Evan nearly laughed at that idea. Mitchell wouldn't be calling him for anything after Evan had told him to go to hell and take his faithless fiancée with him.

But this was his mother, whom he harbored real affection for. His mother, who was always caught in the middle of the tension that existed between him and his father and between him and Mitchell.

"All right, Mom. I'll come. But I'll be bringing someone with me. I hope you don't mind."

He could practically see her beam right through the phone.

"Why, Evan, you didn't tell me you were seeing someone new! Of course you're welcome to bring her. I'll very much look forward to meeting her."

"Can you forward all the details to my assistant so she can make arrangements?"

His mom sighed. "How did I know you wouldn't have kept the original e-mail?"

Because he'd immediately sent it to the trash folder? Of course he wouldn't tell her that.

"Send it to Vickie and I'll see you on Friday. I love you," he said after a short pause.

"I love you too, son. I'm so very glad you're coming."

He ended the call and stared down at his BlackBerry.

Friday. Hell. Friday was when he was meeting Celia. Finally meeting Celia.

He'd planned meticulously, not wanting to seem over-anxious. He'd flirted, exchanged long, seeking glances and had spent a lot of damn time in the shower. He was surprised he hadn't come down with hypothermia.

And now he was going to have to cancel because his mother thought that he should go see the woman he was supposed to have married instead marry his younger brother.

He needed to find a date. Preferably one who would convince his mother he wasn't secretly pining over Bettina. He wasn't. He'd gotten over her the moment she'd dumped him for his brother when Mitchell was appointed the CEO position in their family jewelry business.

She preferred the glitz-and-glamour facade of the jewelry world over the sweaty, athletic image of his company. It was just as well she wasn't bright enough to have done any research. If she had, she would have known that Evan's company's earnings far exceeded those of his father's jewelry business. And it had only taken him a few years to accomplish it.

His mother wouldn't believe it but Evan was grateful to his brother for being a selfish pinhead. Mitchell wanted Bettina because Evan had her. Thanks to that deep need for one-upmanship, Evan had narrowly escaped a huge mistake.

But it didn't mean he wanted to spend quality time with his controlling father and his spoiled, self-indulgent sibling. He'd agreed, however, and now he needed a date.

With a shake of his head, he began scrolling through his address book in his BlackBerry. He had narrowed his options to three women, when the solution came to him.

It was brilliant, really. He was an idiot for not having

thought of it immediately. It certainly solved *all* his problems.

Finally he had a way of luring Celia to him. It would be business, of course, but if the setting happened to be intimate and she was for all practical purposes stranded with him on Catalina Island for three days…

A satisfied smile raised the corners of his mouth. Maybe the wedding wouldn't be such a bad thing after all.

Two

When Celia pulled into her father's driveway, she was relieved to see Noah's Mercedes parked beside their father's pickup. She pulled her black BMW on the other side of the truck and grinned at how the two expensive cars flanked the beat-up old piece of family history.

As she got out, she heard the roar of another engine and turned to see Dalton pull in behind her. To her utter shock, Adam climbed out of the passenger seat.

"Adam!" she exclaimed, and ran straight for him.

He grinned just before she launched herself into his arms. She hit his chest and as she'd known he would, he caught her and whirled her around. Just like he'd done when she'd been five years old and every year since.

"How come I never get greetings like that?" Dalton grumbled as he climbed from behind the wheel.

"I'm so glad to see you," she whispered fiercely.

His big arms surrounded her in a hug that nearly squeezed the breath out of her. Adam always gave the best hugs.

"It's good to see you too, Cece. I missed you. Took you long enough to come back home."

She slid down until her feet met the ground again, and she briefly looked away.

"Hey," he chided as he nudged her chin until she looked at him again. "None of that. It's all in the past, and it's a good damn thing it is, otherwise your brothers would hop the first plane to New York and beat the crap out of your former boss."

"Hey, hello, I'm here, too," Dalton said, waving a hand between them.

She held Adam's gaze for a moment longer and then smiled her thanks. Her brothers were overbearing. They were loud, protective and they certainly had their faults. Like not believing she needed to do anything more in life than look pretty and let them support her. But God love them, they were fierce in their loyalty to her, and she adored them for it.

Finally she turned to Dalton. "You I saw two weekends ago. Adam I haven't seen in forever." She glanced back at Adam. "Why is that anyway?"

He grimaced. "Sorry. Busy time of the year."

She nodded. Adam, her oldest brother, owned a successful landscaping business and spring was always a hectic time. They rarely saw him until the fall when business started to slow.

Dalton slung an arm over Celia's shoulders and planted an affectionate kiss on her cheek. "I see Mr. Baseball is here. Must have caught a break before the season starts."

"You guys going to the season opener?" she asked.

"Wouldn't miss it," Adam said.

"I have a favor to ask then."

Both brothers looked curiously at her.

"I'm bringing a client and I'd like to keep my relationship to Noah on the down low."

Curiosity gleamed in their eyes. She knew they wanted to ask, but when she didn't volunteer her reasons why, they didn't pursue the matter.

"Okay. Not a problem," Adam finally said.

"Are you three going to stand out there all day or are you coming in to eat?"

Her father's voice boomed from the front porch, and

they turned to see him leaning against the doorframe, impatience evident in his stance.

Celia grinned. "We better go in before he starts muttering threats."

Adam ruffled her hair then tucked his arm over her neck so he had her in a headlock. He started toward the house, dragging her with him.

When they got to the porch, she laughingly stumbled from Adam's hold and gave her dad a quick hug. He squeezed her and dropped a kiss on the top of her head.

"Where's Noah?" she asked.

"Where he always is. Parked in front of the big screen, watching baseball."

She slipped past her father while he greeted his sons and entered the home she'd grown up in. When she got to the living room, she saw Noah sprawled in the recliner, remote in hand as he flipped through footage of past baseball games.

"Hey," she called.

He looked up, his eyes warming in welcome. As he got up, he smiled broadly at her then held out his arms.

She hugged him then made a show of feeling his ribs.

"They don't feed you in training camp?"

He laughed. "You know damn well that all I ever do is eat. I think my tapeworms have tapeworms."

She glanced back to make sure they were still alone and then lowered her voice.

"Are you going to hang around later or do you have to be somewhere?"

His eyes narrowed, and he lost the smile.

"I don't have to be anywhere today. Why do you ask?"

"I need to talk to you about something. I have a favor to ask, and I'd rather not get into it in front of everyone."

He frowned now. "Is everything okay, Cece? You in some kind of trouble? Do I need to kill anyone?"

She rolled her eyes. "You're too valuable to go to prison. You'd have Dalton do it anyway."

Noah smirked. "The pretty boy would be popular in prison."

"You're a sick puppy. And no, nothing's wrong. Promise. Just want to run something by you that could be beneficial to us both."

"Okay, if you're going to be all mysterious on me. I guess I can wait until later. You want to go back to your place for a while? I'd invite you to mine but the maid quit on me last week and it's not a pretty sight. You do have food, right?"

She shook her head. "Yes, I have food, and yes, we can go back to my place. For God's sake, Noah, how hard is it to pick up after yourself? Or if you can't do that, at least pick up the phone and get another maid service?"

"I've sort of been blackballed," he mumbled. "I have to find an agency where my reputation hasn't preceded me."

"I feel so sorry for the woman you marry. She'll be in ten kinds of hell."

"You don't have to worry because that's not going to happen."

"Sure. Okay. I believe you."

They both looked up when the others spilled into the living room. Noah gave her arm a light squeeze and mouthed "later."

"Food'll be on the table in fifteen minutes," her father announced.

Her mouth watered. She didn't even know what her dad had cooked. It didn't matter. The man was a culinary genius.

Lunch was a rambunctious affair. Her brothers bickered and joked endlessly while her father looked on indulgently. She'd missed all of this during her years in New York. Though she loathed the circumstances that brought her home, she was glad to be back in the comforting circle of her family. Even if they were all just a generation from knuckles-dragging-on-the-ground cavemen.

After the table had been cleared, the argument started over what channel the television landed on. Noah didn't know anything but ESPN or the Food Network existed, Dalton liked anything that was mindless, particularly if explosions were involved, and Adam liked to torment his brothers by forcing them to watch gardening shows.

Celia settled back to enjoy the sights and sounds of home. Her father sat on the couch next to her and shook his head over his sons' antics.

It was the truth, she'd fled the hovering overprotectiveness of her family. She'd been determined to make her mark on the world while they wanted her to stay home, where they could support her and look out for her.

She wasn't a vain woman, but she knew men found her attractive. She was probably considered beautiful by most, but her looks had been the cause of a lot of problems in her life.

Because of her delicate looks, her brothers and even her father thought her job was just to look pretty and let them provide for her. She hadn't been encouraged to go to college—she'd done all of that on her own—and they certainly hadn't wanted her to have a career in something as demanding as advertising.

She'd ignored their objections. She'd gotten her degree and after graduation, she'd taken a job in New York City. After a couple of years, she'd taken a position with a large, prestigious firm. She was on her way up. A promotion had just cemented her triumph. And then it had all come crashing down like a bridge in an earthquake.

Adam rising from his chair shook her from her angry thoughts. She forced her fingers to relax and winced at the marks she'd left on her palms.

"Leaving already?" she asked.

Adam pulled her up into a bear hug. "Yeah. I need to check on a job. I'll see you at the season opener, though."

She kissed his cheek and patted his shoulder affectionately. "Of course."

She turned to Dalton. "I guess you'll be going, too, since you brought him over."

"Yep. I have a date I've got to get ready for anyway."

No one seemed surprised by that announcement.

"I'll walk you guys out. I need to run, too. I have a pitch to prepare for."

Her father grimaced, and she steeled herself for another gruff lecture about how she worked too hard. An interesting statement since Adam worked harder than all of them, and no one ever lectured him.

To her surprise, he remained silent. She regarded him with a raised eyebrow and wondered if he'd burst at the seams, but his lips remained in a firm line. He rose from the couch to hug her and then gruffly reminded her to be sure and get enough rest.

They all walked out together, and her father reminded them all of lunch next Sunday. Celia waved to Adam and Dalton before climbing into her car. Noah stood, saying his goodbyes to their father, and she drove down the driveway. Noah would be along shortly and she needed to make sure her pantry would survive the assault.

Celia had just done a cursory examination of her stock of food—cursing the fact she hadn't been to the market in far too long—when the door buzzer sounded.

She strode across to the call box and mashed the button. "That you, Noah?"

"Yep, buzz me in?"

A few seconds later, Noah walked in, and she smiled her welcome.

"I know that smile," he said suspiciously. "That's a smile that says you lured me here under false pretenses. You don't have any food, do you?"

"Weeeell, no. But I did just order pizza."

"You're forgiven, but I refuse to have a reasonable discussion until it gets here."

She laughed and punched him on the arm when he flopped on the sofa next to her. "If I didn't need a favor from you, I'd make you pay for it."

His expression grew serious. "So what is this favor, anyway?"

"Oh, no. I'm not asking you for anything until you have a full stomach. Again, since you ate not even three hours ago."

He grunted but didn't offer any argument. His stomach was too important.

He reached for the remote and flipped on the TV. A few seconds later, the sports recap was on, and he settled back against the couch.

The pizza didn't take long—thanks to the bistro right around the corner offering delivery service. Soon the decadent smells of a completely loaded pizza filled her apartment. Despite all she'd eaten at lunch, her stomach growled in anticipation. She eyed the gooey dripping cheese and grimaced. It might taste good, but it would go straight to her hips. Then again, that's what the treadmill was for.

She dropped the box on the coffee table in front of Noah, not bothering with plates. He eyed the mountain of toppings with something akin to bliss.

She waited until he'd grabbed the first piece before she carefully took a slice and nibbled on the end. It was, in a word, sheer heaven. She leaned back and waited for Noah to down the first slice. When he was on his second, he turned and said around a mouthful of pizza, "So what's this favor you need?"

She sat forward, putting half the slice down on a napkin.

"I have this client…well he's a client I want to land. Evan Reese."

Noah stopped chewing. "The guy who sells athletic wear?"

She nodded. "Yeah. He fired his last agency and has yet to sign with a new one. I want him. Maddox Communications wants him."

"Okay. So where do I fit into the picture?"

For a moment her nerve deserted her, and then she mentally slapped herself upside the head. In her profession there was no room for the spineless. She hadn't worked her way into the confidence of Brock Maddox acting like a jellyfish.

"I want you to agree to front his new line of athletic wear."

Noah blinked then he frowned, and finally he put down his half-eaten slice. For a moment he was quiet. She waited, fully expecting him to say no or to launch into all the reasons why he didn't take endorsement deals. She knew them all. But he did none of those things. Instead he studied her carefully, his gaze sliding over her features as though he was reaching right into her head and pulling out her every thought.

He wouldn't ask why him. He was a huge name in baseball, and he was more sought after than any other professional athlete mainly because of his refusal to take endorsement deals. Instead of deterring companies, it made them all the more determined to be the first to lure Noah Hart to their brand.

She could beg. She could hurry through a prepared explanation as to why she needed him, but she wasn't going to wheedle and cajole.

Noah was still frowning as he studied her. "This is important to you."

She nodded. "Evan is a big client. My boss is trusting me to land the account. Don't get me wrong, I'll get him with or without you, but you'd be the nail in his coffin. Plus it would be huge for you. Reese will pay a lot to have you be the spokesman for his sportswear."

Noah sighed. "I wish you'd just quit this job. You don't have to work, and you know it. You don't have to prove yourself to anyone, Cece. Certainly not to your family. Adam, Dalton and I make more than enough money to support you. It would make Dad happy if you didn't have such a stressful job. He's convinced you'll have an ulcer before you're thirty."

She smiled faintly. "I am thirty."

He shot her an impatient look.

"Look, Noah, would you quit baseball just because your brothers make enough money to support you? They do, you know."

A derisive, strangling sound rose from his throat. He licked his lips as if to rid himself of a really bad taste.

"It's different."

"I know, I know. You're a man, and I'm a woman." Her lips curled in disgust. "Noah, I love you dearly. You're the best brother a girl could ask for. But you're a chauvinist to your toes."

He huffed but didn't dispute her accusation. Then his expression grew thoughtful again. "I assume you've done your research on this man and his company."

Celia nodded before he'd even finished. On the surface, Noah looked and acted laissez-faire. He had all the appearances of a golden-boy jock whose only concern might be fast cars and faster women. But beneath that illusion lay a man who had a deep social conscience.

His refusal of endorsement deals had gained him a reputation of eccentricity from some. Others regarded him incredulously as a fool to pass on the opportunity to make millions by doing nothing more than lend his name to countless companies willing to part with their dollars for his endorsement. But the simple fact was that Noah did meticulous research on all the corporations that approached him, and so far none had passed muster with him.

"E-mail it all to me. I'll take a look. If it checks out, I'm willing to listen to his offer."

She leaned over and kissed his cheek. "Thanks, Noah. You're the best."

"I don't suppose you'll be so grateful that you'll volunteer to clean my apartment?"

She snorted and picked up her slice of pizza again. "Put it this way. I'd rather quit my job and let you and Adam support me than clean your place."

He winced. "Well, damn. No need to be so mean about it."

"Poor baby. Oh, hey, I need one more favor."

His eyes narrowed, and he glared at her. "You just turn down my request for you to play cleaning lady and you insult me in the process and then have the cheek to want another favor?"

"How about I find you a replacement cleaning service? Then both of us are happy."

He got a hopeful puppy dog look that would probably make mush of most women. Thankfully she was his sister and completely immune to any adorableness on his part.

"Okay, you find me someone to clear a path in my apartment and whatever this other favor of yours is I'll do it."

"Wow—and you don't even know what it is."

"Should tell you how desperate I am," he muttered.

She laughed and punched him in the arm. "All I need are two very cushy seats behind home plate for the season opener. I'll be taking Evan. Hopefully."

"Anyone ever tell you how expensive you are?"

"Hey, wait a second. A minute ago, you were trying to convince me to quit my job so you could support me."

His expression went from teasing to serious with one blink. "I just worry about you, Cece. That's all. What happened in New York would have never occurred if—"

She stiffened and held her hand, halting him in midsentence. "I don't want to talk about New York."

Regret flashed in his eyes. "Sorry. Consider it dropped."

She waited for her pulse to settle and then she forced a smile. "So you'll take a look at the research I've compiled? You'll like Reese. He's a veritable Boy Scout. His employees love him. He has a cracking health-insurance plan. He's had no layoffs since his business started and he's not shipping jobs or production overseas. Let's see. What else? He's a regular contributor to a half dozen pet charities—"

Noah held up his hands in surrender. "Okay, okay, he's a saint. I get it. How do other men ever measure up?"

"Cut the sarcasm."

He checked his watch and let out a sigh. "Sorry to break this up so early, especially since I haven't finished the pizza. *Somebody* talked too much. Very distracting. E-mail me the stuff. I'll take a look. And the tickets will be waiting for you at the box office."

"You always were my favorite sibling," she said affectionately.

He dropped a kiss on top of her head then stood and stretched lazily.

"I'll give you a call when I'm through reading everything."

Three

Evan walked into the suite of offices he leased for the times he was in San Francisco. It wasn't home, and though Union Square was a sumptuous neighborhood that catered to upscale businesses, he preferred the funky modern feel of Seattle.

He nodded a good morning to his receptionist but halted when she came out of her seat, a concerned expression on her face.

"You shouldn't go in there," Tanya said in a hushed whisper.

He raised an eyebrow when he realized she was gesturing toward his office.

"Why the devil not?" he demanded.

She put one hand up to shield her mouth and then she tapped her finger against her palm—in the direction of his office.

"Because *she's* in there."

Evan turned to stare down the hall toward his office, but the door was closed. Damn, but he didn't have time for this. He looked back at Tanya and tried to stifle his growing impatience. The girl was highly efficient if a little eccentric. But he liked unconventional, and while she'd probably fit in better with his Seattle staff with her colored hair, multiple piercings and vintage 1930s clothing, he found she brought a sort of vibrancy to an otherwise stuffy office here.

"Okay, Tanya. First of all, who the hell is 'she' and where is Vickie?"

It wasn't like Vickie not to meet him as he got off the elevator. His longtime assistant traveled with him everywhere. She had an apartment here and in Seattle. She had an uncanny knack for knowing precisely when he'd show up, and as a result she was always there, ready to pelt him with the day's obligations.

Tanya's face fell. "Oh, sir, did you not get your message? I left you two. Vickie's granddaughter was rushed to the hospital early this morning. They suspect appendicitis. She's in surgery now."

Evan frowned. "No, I didn't get any such message. Keep me updated. I want to know the minute she's out of surgery. Send flowers and make sure Vickie has everything she might need. On second thought, send over food for the family. Hospital food is terrible. And arrange for a hospitality suite. If there is a hotel close to the hospital, have a block of rooms set aside for any of the family members."

Tanya blinked then hurriedly picked up a notepad and began scribbling.

Evan waited a moment then sighed. "Tanya?"

She looked up, blinking, as if surprised to still see him standing there.

"Who is the 'she' waiting in my office?"

Tanya's nose curled in distaste. "It's Miss Hammond, sir. I couldn't stop her. She was quite imperious. Told me she'd wait for you."

It was all Evan could do not to look heavenward and ask "why me?" He glanced down the hall and briefly considered leaving. He had no patience for Bettina today, and after his mother had extracted his promise to attend this weekend's debacle, he couldn't imagine anything Bettina could have to say to him.

"Keep me posted on Vickie's granddaughter," he said as he turned to go down to his office.

He opened the door and swept in, his gaze immediately finding Bettina. She was sitting on one of the sofas lining the window that overlooked the outdoor cafés lining the sidewalk below.

"Bettina," he said as he tossed his briefcase onto his desk. "What brings you here?"

Bettina rose, her hands going down to smooth her dress. The motion directed attention to her legs—her self-admitted favorite personal attribute. The dress stopped almost at midthigh, which meant quite a lot of those legs were on display.

Evan wouldn't lie. He'd enjoyed those legs. It was just too bad they were attached to the rest of her.

Her expression creased into one of fake pain. She crossed the room, holding her hands dramatically in front of her to grasp his.

"I wanted to thank you for agreeing to come to the wedding. It means the world to Mitchell and your mom and dad. I know how painful it must be. I can't imagine how difficult it was for you to agree to go after I broke your heart."

Evan just stared at her. Part of him wanted to ask her what planet she existed on, but he already knew the answer to that. It was planet Bettina, where everything revolved around her. Did she honestly believe he was still pining for her?

"Cut the theatrics, Bettina. Why are you really here? You don't care if I show up or not, so why pretend otherwise? In fact, I'd be willing to admit you hoped I wouldn't."

She blinked, and for a moment he saw bitterness in her eyes.

"Lucy said you were bringing a...date. It was clever of you, really. But you don't fool me, Evan. Everyone knows you haven't been serious about anyone since me. Who is she? Someone you've met socially? Do you know anything about her? Does she know she's going as an accessory? God knows that's all I ever was to you."

"You can't have it both ways, Bettina. Either I was serious about you or you were an accessory," he drawled. "Which is it?"

She flushed angrily. "I only meant that you haven't dated any woman more than once since I broke things off with you."

He made an exaggerated expression of surprise. "You flatter me. I had no idea you were so interested in who I date. I would have thought my brother kept you too occupied to monitor my love life."

"Bring your date, Evan. But you know and I know she isn't me. She'll never be me. Don't think you'll take anything away from my wedding day."

With that she stalked out of his office, leaving Evan to shake his head. He really ought to call his brother and thank him profusely.

He sank into his chair and opened his day planner. Vickie kept meticulous records of all appointments for just such rare occasions that she was out of pocket. He frowned when he saw his calendar was full. Except for one forty-five-minute window for lunch.

His mind immediately went to Celia. Celia, whose office was just two blocks from his. He'd planned to call her, but a proposition such as he had in mind was really better delivered in person. He wouldn't have a lot of time, and he doubted she had much free time, either, but he knew without arrogance that if he asked her to lunch, she wouldn't refuse. She wanted his business too badly.

He hit the button to call Vickie then quickly remembered she wasn't there. He connected to Tanya instead.

"Yes, sir?"

"Tanya, I need Celia Taylor of Maddox Communications on the phone."

Celia stepped out of the elevator and was met with a cheerful hello from Shelby, the receptionist for Maddox Communications. Shelby was young and friendly. She also had superb organization skills and a memory like a steel trap. Which made her a perfect asset. But more importantly, she knew everything about everyone at Maddox. There wasn't a piece of juicy gossip floating around that Shelby didn't know, and she didn't mind sharing it. Celia found it useful to keep in the know. Never again would she be caught off guard like she'd been in her last job.

"Good morning, Shelby," Celia returned as she paused in front of Shelby's desk. "Any messages for me?"

Shelby's eyes twinkled and she leaned forward to whisper conspiratorially. "Latest rumors that have surfaced are about the boss man and his assistant."

Celia frowned. "You mean, him and Elle?"

Elle didn't seem like the type to indulge in a torrid office affair and definitely not with her boss. Celia felt compelled to warn Elle about the potential pitfalls of even having such a rumor circulate, but it was just a rumor, and Elle might not appreciate Celia broaching the subject.

Shelby shrugged. "Well, they do seem to spend a lot of time together."

"Of course they do. She's his assistant," Celia pointed out.

"I just repeat what others are saying."

Celia gripped her briefcase a little tighter. It wouldn't do her any good to get involved. Brock and Elle were adults. She just hoped Elle wasn't hurt by the idle gossip.

"Hey, Shelby," Celia began as she remembered why she'd stopped to begin with. "I need you to look up a cleaning service." She dug around in her briefcase then pulled out a sheet of paper that had all the names of the agencies Noah had already contacted. She handed it over the counter to Shelby. "These are the ones marked off the list of possibilities. I need you to make it clear this is a demanding client and that he's a slob through and through. Money is no object but whoever the poor soul is who takes the job will definitely earn their paycheck."

Shelby's eyes widened. "Noah Hart. *The* Noah Hart? He needs a housekeeper? I'm available. I mean, I can totally quit here, right?"

Celia shot her a "get real" look. "Let me know if you find someone. Oh, and I'm expecting a call from Evan Reese's assistant. I don't care what I'm doing or who I'm with, make sure I get that call."

As she walked away, Shelby called out to her. "Hey, wait. How do you know Noah Hart? He's not a client of Maddox."

Celia smiled and kept walking toward her office. Normally she'd stop in on some of her coworkers, say hello, get a feel for what the day's events were, but she was already running late, thanks to a breakfast meeting going well into the brunch hour. She needed to play catch-up on phone messages and e-mails before a full afternoon of client calls and a staff meeting to close out the day.

She'd made a sizeable dent in the backlog of messages when her interoffice intercom buzzed.

"Celia, Mr. Reese is on line two."

Celia frowned. "Mr. Reese himself or Mr. Reese's assistant?"

"Mr. Reese."

"Put him through," she said crisply.

She wiped her hand on her skirt then shook her head. What did she have to be nervous about? As soon as the phone rang, she picked it up.

"Celia Taylor."

"Celia, how are you?"

Even his voice sent a bolt of awareness through her body. When would she stop acting like a teenage girl in the throes of her first sexual awakening? It was ridiculous. It wasn't professional.

"I'm good, Evan. And you?"

"I don't have a lot of time. I wanted to meet for lunch today. That is, if your schedule permits?"

There was a note of confidence in his voice. He knew damn well she wouldn't say no. Hastily, she checked the clock.

"What time?"

"Now."

Panic scuttled around her stomach. Now? She wasn't prepared to meet him now. Surely he didn't want to reschedule their informal pitch session from Friday to now?

"I thought we had a lunch date on Friday?"

She was stalling as her brain scrambled to catch up.

"I want to discuss Friday today. There's been a change of plans."

Her heart sank. There was no way she could have her act together right now.

"I only have forty-five minutes," he continued. "We're two blocks apart. Shall we meet in the middle? Our choices are French, Italian or good ole American."

"I'm up for anything," she said faintly.

She propped the phone between her shoulder and her ear and began frantically digging for her notes on his account. She stuffed everything into a folder and reached for her briefcase.

"Great. Shall we meet in say five minutes? I'll start out now."

"Sure, meet you there."

He hung up and for a moment she stood there like a

moron, the phone still stuck to her ear. Then she slammed it down, took in a deep steadying breath and declared battle.

She could do this in her sleep.

Slinging the bag over her shoulder, she all but jogged out of her office and down the hallway.

She passed Ash Williams, Maddox's CFO, who held up a finger and opened his mouth to say something to her.

"Not now, Ash," she called as she hustled by. "Late for an important lunch date."

She didn't even look to see his reaction.

She ran past Shelby and hollered back as she punched the button for the elevator.

"If Brock asks, I'm having lunch with Mr. Reese. Just tell him Friday got moved up. If anyone else asks, just tell them I'll return this afternoon."

The elevator opened and she ducked in. As she turned around, she saw Shelby's look of befuddlement just as the doors slid shut again.

When she reached the lobby, she stopped in the bathroom long enough to check her appearance. She wouldn't stop traffic for sure, but at least she didn't look as frazzled as she felt.

The heels she'd chosen to complete her outfit were fabulous—as long as she didn't have to actually walk in them. A trek down the block on uneven cement sidewalks wasn't what she had in mind. She kept tennis shoes in her office for just such occasions, but five minutes notice on the most important lunch date of her career didn't give her time to worry over footwear. She'd just suck it up.

When she crossed the street to the next block, she realized she never had gotten where they were supposed to meet. Italian, French or American. Her gaze scanned the bright umbrellas scattered along the sidewalk cafés, first on her side of the street and then across.

A vacuum formed, sucking all the oxygen right out of

her lungs the moment she laid eyes on him. He stood in the sunlight, one hand shoved into the pocket of his slacks, the other holding a phone to his ear.

Power. There was an aura of power that surrounded him, and it drew her like a magnet. For a moment, she just stood watching him in absolute girly delight. He was simply…delicious looking.

Then he turned slightly and found her. How, she wasn't sure given how busy the street was, but he locked onto her immediately almost as if he'd sensed her perusal.

She straightened and started forward, embarrassed to have been caught staring.

She crossed the street, hugging her briefcase between her arm and her side. Evan watched her approach, lean hunger gleaming in his eyes. His features relaxed into a smile as she drew abreast of him.

"Right on time."

She nodded, not wanting to betray how out of breath she was from her flight from her office.

"I chose good ole American," he said as he gestured toward a nearby table. "I hope that was all right."

"Of course."

He held out his arm for her to precede him to the table at the end of the row. She sat, grateful to be off her feet, and placed her briefcase beside her.

He took his seat across from her and motioned for the waiter.

"Would you like wine?" Evan asked Celia when the waiter approached.

"Whatever you're having is fine."

Evan relayed his request and then looked over at Celia. "I asked you to lunch because I'm afraid something has come up and we won't be able to make our lunch date on Friday."

She nodded then reached down for her briefcase. "That's

all right. I brought along the information I wanted to present—"

He reached over and circled her wrist with his fingers. "That isn't why I invited you to lunch."

She blinked and let go of her briefcase.

"I'd still like to keep our appointment… I'd just like to change the location."

She was royally confused now, and it must have shown. Amusement twinkled in his eyes and he smiled.

"I don't have a lot of time today, so let me come straight to the point."

His fingers were still around her wrist, though they'd loosened, and his thumb moved idly over her pulse point. She was sure her pulse was racing. It probably felt like a train under his fingers. She didn't move. Didn't even breathe. She didn't want to lose the marvelous sensation of his touch. Did he have any idea just how devastating his effect on her was?

"I have a wedding this weekend." She could swear his lips curled in distaste. "A family wedding. My brother is getting married on Catalina Island. I'm to be there Thursday evening, hence the reason I can't make our Friday meeting."

"I understand," she said. "We can reschedule at your convenience."

"I'd like you to go with me."

Before she could call back the reaction, her eyes widened and she pulled her hand from his. She put it in her lap and cupped her other hand over it, wanting to preserve the sensation of his fingers over hers.

He put up his hand in an impatient gesture then lowered it and fiddled with the napkin on the table. He seemed almost uneasy. She cocked her head, curious now as to what he would say next.

"My schedule is quite busy. I need to move on this new

campaign. I can't spare weeks searching for a new agency. If you went with me, I could listen to your ideas. I realize a wedding isn't ideal. I'd rather be just about any other place myself."

Though it certainly wasn't voiced as a threat, it was certainly implied. If she went with him, he'd listen to her pitch. If she didn't he might not have time for her when he returned.

Worry knotted her stomach. Tagging along to a family wedding seemed entirely too personal even if the purpose was solely business. Not to mention it was hard enough to battle her attraction for him in a business setting. But something as intimate as a wedding?

"How long would we be…away?"

The question came out more as a squeak than a concise, professional query. She sounded like a scared little girl facing the big bad wolf. Oh, but Evan made such a yummy wolf.

It was all she could do not to put her head on the table and bang a few times.

"We'd fly out Thursday evening. Rehearsal and dinner on Friday, wedding Saturday with reception to follow and since it will likely go well into the night, we'd return Sunday."

It would only require one missed day of work. No one but Brock would even need to know, and he certainly wouldn't spill the beans.

She didn't know why she hadn't immediately agreed. She couldn't afford to say no. He had her over a barrel and he damn well knew it. Still, she hesitated—if for no other reason than to let him know he didn't call all the shots.

Okay, so maybe he did, but it didn't hurt him to think otherwise. For two seconds.

"All right," she said in as level a voice as she could manage.

Did he expect her to attend the festivities? It certainly sounded as though he did by the way he outlined the events. She supposed it would be rude to tag along and lurk in the shadows waiting for her appointed time. Or maybe he envisioned having her follow him around everywhere so he could fit in snatches of conversation when possible.

"I'd be happy to purchase any items you may need for the trip," he said.

Startled, she glanced up. "No, I mean…no. Of course not. I can manage just fine. You'll need to tell me the appropriate dress code of course."

He managed a wry smile. "I'm sure anything to do with Bettina will be formal. Quite formal with lots of glitter and fanfare."

His gaze slid sensuously over her features and then lower until her neck heated with a blush.

"I think anything you wear will be stunning. The dress you wore the other night was perfection on you."

The blush climbed higher and she prayed her cheeks didn't look like twin torches.

"I'm sure I can find something glitzy and glamorous," she said lightly. "We girls do like the opportunity to play dress up."

Interest sparked in his eyes. "I can't wait."

The waiter returned with the wine, and Celia latched gratefully onto the glass. Her hands shook. She was sure if she stood, she'd go down like a brick. She'd break an ankle trying to stay up on these ridiculous heels.

Note to self: Don't pack gorgeous, sexy shoes for the weekend. Around him, she'd be a disaster on stilts. He'd spend his entire time picking her up off the floor, that is if she didn't end up in the hospital in traction.

"I'll call you later in the week with the flight arrangements. We'll be taking my private jet."

She swallowed and nodded, then realizing he'd need her

number—her cell number and not her office number—she reached down into her briefcase to retrieve a business card.

She frowned, fumbled some more then pulled the bag into her lap. With a groan she realized her business-card holder must have fallen out. Impatiently she tore a piece of paper off a notepad and took out her pen.

Dropping the bag again, she put the paper on the table and hastily scribbled her home and cell number then passed it across the table to Evan.

He took it, studied it a moment then carefully folded it and tucked it away in the breast pocket of his jacket. The waiter approached with menus and Evan looked to her for her order.

"Just the lunch salad," she said. What she really wanted was a really greasy burger with onion rings, but she didn't want to appall Evan. Her brothers gave her all sorts of hell for her indelicate tastes, but then they were to blame for them.

Evan ordered a steak, medium, and after the waiter was gone, Evan stared over at her, his gaze inquisitive.

She cocked her head, prepared for him to ask her a question, but he didn't say anything. He just seemed to study her as if he wanted to uncover all her deep, dark secrets.

Finally he sat back with a satisfied smile. His eyes glinted with triumph.

"I think this wedding is going to turn out to be enjoyable after all."

Four

Celia stepped off the elevator and walked by Shelby, who held her hand up to get Celia's attention.

"Later, Shelby," she called as she headed for Brock's office.

When she got to his door, she was nearly run over as Ash came out. He sidestepped her and kept on walking, his forehead wrinkled as if he were lost in thought. She wasn't even sure he'd seen her.

She stuck her head in Brock's door and breathed a sigh of relief when she found him alone. He glanced up and motioned her in.

"What's with him?" she asked, jerking her head over her shoulder in Ash's direction. "He's been weird lately."

Brock gave her one of those puzzled male looks that suggested he didn't have a clue what she was talking about. She rolled her eyes. Ash had been walking around in a fog, which wasn't typical. He was usually on top of everything and everyone. Celia had overheard Shelby talking about a falling-out with a girlfriend, but then she hadn't even known Ash had been seeing anyone. Not that he would have confided in her.

She didn't bother sitting. She had too much to do, and this wouldn't take long.

"I have to go out of town Thursday afternoon."

Brock stared back at her for a moment and then his brows drew together. He frowned and dropped the pen he'd been fiddling with.

"Is this some kind of emergency? You're supposed to meet with Evan Reese on Friday."

His tone suggested someone better be dying. He opened his mouth to say more but before he got off on the tangent she knew was coming, she held up her hand.

"I just had lunch with Evan. There's been a change in plans. He has to be at some family wedding this weekend in Catalina so he couldn't make it on Friday. He said he wants to move on this campaign and he doesn't have a lot of time to spend in the selection process."

Brock swore, his face going red. He picked the pen back up and flung it across his desk. "Dammit, is he even going to listen to our pitch?"

She sucked in a breath. "He wants me to go to Catalina with him. We'd leave Thursday afternoon. It's the only time he can spare me and he's promised to listen to my ideas while we're there."

Brock's brow furrowed further and he studied her intently. "I see."

Forgetting about all she needed to do and that she didn't want to be stuck here in Brock's office forever, she sank down into one of the chairs and stared glumly at her boss.

"I told him I'd go. I didn't see that I had a choice. While he didn't come out and say it, he implied that if I didn't, he was prepared to go with another agency."

"I agree you should go. Does that make me an ass?"

Celia laughed, some of the tension leaving her shoulders. "No, it doesn't make you an ass. I guess I just worry about the fallout. It's stupid. I shouldn't care. I never would have before, but I know what will be said if it gets out and how things will be twisted."

"You have my support, Celia, and you have the support of the agency. Don't ever doubt that."

She rose and smiled gratefully at him. "Thank you, Brock."

He grunted. "Get me the damn account. That's all the thanks I need."

She stopped on her way out, put her hand on the door frame and looked back. "I'll need someone to cover for me on Friday. I have two client appointments, one in the morning and one in the afternoon."

"Jason will cover for you. You just worry about knocking Evan Reese's socks off."

"I will," Celia murmured. "I will."

On her way down the hall, her BlackBerry rang and she dug into the pocket of her briefcase for it. Seeing Noah's number on the LCD, she mashed the answer button and stuck the phone to her ear as she walked into her office.

"I'm working on the maid service," she said in lieu of hello.

Noah chuckled. "Great, I nearly killed myself getting out of bed this morning. You'd be amazed how dangerous a pair of dirty underwear can be."

Her nose wrinkled in disgust. "Would you at least try not to send the maid screaming from your house on her first day? That's just gross."

He made a derisive sound. "So I read through the info you sent. I also had my agent do some checking. I might add that my agent is orgasmic that I'm considering this endorsement deal."

"Tell him I expect a nice Christmas gift as thank you," Celia said.

"Oh, please. He doesn't even give his mother presents."

Usually she wouldn't mind chatting mindlessly with her siblings, but she had a hundred things to do before Thursday, including figure out how she was going to survive a weekend on an island with a man who made mincemeat of her willpower.

"So does this mean you'll consider it?"

There was a pause, and she found herself holding her breath.

"Yeah. He checks out. He seems as solid as you said he was. I'll talk to him if nothing else."

She did a double-fist pump and dropped her bag on the floor by her desk.

"Have his people call my people," Noah said airily.

Celia laughed. "I am his people. Or at least I will be."

"Hey, you going to be at Dad's this weekend?"

She winced when she remembered that she'd told their father she would indeed be there for Sunday dinner again.

"Afraid not. Something's come up."

Noah made a disapproving sound. "Don't you ever take off? It's Sunday, for Pete's sake."

"How do you know it's work?" she defended. "Maybe I have a hot date."

He snorted. "When was the last time you went on a hot date? It's always work with you."

Knowing they were about to get into lecture territory again, Celia cut him off before he got carried away.

"Hey, I have to run, Noah. Have a meeting in five minutes. I'll call you later, okay?"

Before he could call her a liar, she hung up and plopped into her chair. She blew out a long sigh of relief and closed her eyes.

It was all coming together. Not without a few potholes, but it was within reach. All she had to do was hold it together and get through the weekend and the account would be hers.

"Knock, knock."

Celia opened her eyes to see Jason Reagart standing in her doorway.

"Brock told me I needed to cover for you on Friday, so I stopped by so you could get me up to speed on what I need to know."

"Yeah, have a seat. Give me a minute. Been running all morning. I'll dig out my notes."

Jason eased into a chair, his long legs eating up most of the space between it and her desk. Celia picked up her beleaguered briefcase and opened it on her desk.

"So how is Lauren?"

She hated idle conversation, but the silence was more awkward and she hadn't planned on having to turn over the two meetings to anyone, so her notes were haphazard at best.

"Pregnant. Grumpy. You know, typical pregnant woman."

Celia scowled at him over the top of her briefcase. "Like you wouldn't be if you had to deal with water retention, hormones and arrogant men?"

Jason laughed. "Hey, I spoil her rotten."

"As you should. Ah, here we go."

She pulled out a folder and tossed it to Jason.

"Everything you need to know for the morning meeting is on pages one through three. This isn't a big deal. They just need a little hand holding and a little ego stroking. Bowl them over with how Maddox is going to make them look good while increasing their exposure by three hundred percent and they'll be fine."

Jason flipped through the pages, his brow creased in concentration. She felt comfortable leaving her clients in his very capable hands. He took his job very seriously and moreover, he was damn good at what he did. Maddox had landed a huge account thanks to him, and if Celia had her way, she was going to top that by landing Evan Reese.

"And the afternoon meeting?" Jason asked.

"Hopefully you can read my notes. I have the Power-Point presentation ready to go. They need to view it and sign off or suggest any changes so we can move it into the production stage. Impress upon them that this is their last chance to see it before it goes nationwide so make sure they're happy with it."

He nodded and straightened the papers before closing the folder. "Don't worry. I'll take care of it. Brock said you were going to be out of town. Hope everything is all right."

There was a subtle question there, and she knew he hoped she'd expound on her reasons for not being there on Friday. She was just grateful Brock hadn't told him where she was going and why.

She smiled. "Everything's fine, and thank you again for stepping in on such short notice. I owe you one. Send Lauren my love. I'll have to remember to buy her a gift certificate from my favorite spa. I can't think of a pregnant woman alive who wouldn't appreciate a massage."

Jason sent her a disgruntled look. "I don't want some beefcake putting his hands on my wife."

Celia rolled her eyes. "The poor woman can't see her feet and is probably miserable, and you're going to be picky about who gives her some relief?"

"Damn right I am!"

Celia made a shooing motion with her hands. "Out. I have work to do."

And she made a mental note to call her salon and make an appointment for Lauren. She'd ask for the hunkiest massage therapist they had.

Five

The car that Evan had sent to collect Celia pulled up to the plane parked on the paved landing area that led to the single runway and stopped just a few feet from where the door to the jet lay open.

Celia looked out the window to see Evan standing a short distance away. He was waiting for her.

The driver opened her door, and she stepped into the afternoon sun. She blinked a few times then pulled her shades from her head over her eyes. Maybe then it wouldn't be so obvious how she ate Evan up with her gaze.

He was dressed casually. Jeans, polo shirt and loafers. She'd only ever seen him in suits, and she hadn't imagined he could look better. She was wrong. So, so wrong.

The jeans cupped him in all the right places. They clung to his thighs, rounded his butt and molded to his groin. They weren't new, starchy-looking jeans, either. They were faded and worn, just like a good pair of jeans should be.

"Celia," he said with a nod as she approached. "If you're ready, we can be on our way."

"I just need to get my luggage…"

She turned to see that the driver was handing her luggage to a uniformed man.

"Okay then, I'm ready," she said cheerfully.

He smiled and motioned for her to precede him onto the plane. She mounted the steps and ducked inside.

Her eyes widened at the luxurious interior. It was simple and understated, but she recognized it for what it was.

Very expensive comfort. She shoved her shades up so she could get a better look.

There was nothing gaudy about any of the furnishings. It looked very masculine. It even smelled masculine. Leather and suede. Earth tones.

Beyond the three rows of seats, there was a small sitting area with a couch and one chair with a coffee table and a television. To her left between the seats and the cockpit was a small galley area complete with a steward.

The older man smiled at her and welcomed her on board.

As she and Evan took their seats, the steward introduced himself as William and asked her if she wanted a drink.

She glanced at Evan then back at William. "Do you have wine?"

William smiled. "But of course. Mr. Reese keeps the airplane stocked with all the necessities."

She'd agree that wine was very necessary.

A few moments later, William returned with two glasses of wine.

"The pilot wished me to tell you he is ready for takeoff at your convenience."

Evan took the glasses and offered one to Celia.

"Tell him I'm ready."

"Very good, sir. I'll close the doors and we'll take off shortly."

"Comfortable?" Evan asked Celia.

She settled back into her seat and sipped at her wine. "Mmm, very. Nice jet."

She should have sat across the aisle from him, but that would be rude since he'd chosen the seat next to her. His nearness was killing her, though. His scent drifted enticingly across her nostrils and she could *feel* his heat. When he moved, his arm brushed against hers, and short of shifting in her seat—which would be terribly obvious—

there was no escaping him. Furthermore, she didn't really want to.

It was on the tip of her tongue to suggest they use the time on the flight to go over her ideas, but she couldn't bring herself to have business intrude.

She mentally shook herself. Intrude on what? This wasn't some romantic getaway. It *was* business. Only business and nothing else.

It was unfair that she should be attracted to someone who was a solid no in her rule book. She'd never broken that unspoken rule. She had never been tempted to get involved with someone she worked with, or worse— a client. It didn't matter, though, because she'd carry the stigma of someone who advanced her career by bestowing sexual favors.

The memory sent rage curdling through her veins. She had to work at keeping her fingers relaxed. She'd worked damn hard to go beyond her family's expectations. And to have it all taken away by someone in a position of power over her made her head explode.

The advertising community was small, and gossip was rampant. She was under no illusion that fleeing New York made it possible for her to leave what happened behind. It hadn't been private. It had been very, very public.

She knew speculation ran wild. She knew people talked. Knew her coworkers probably whispered behind her back and pondered the possibility that she'd slept with Brock or Flynn Maddox to secure her position in the agency and to be granted the opportunity to land Evan Reese's account. They probably thought she'd do whatever it took to persuade Evan.

The only person she'd bothered to defend herself to was Brock, and she figured she owed him that much if he was going to hire her. Only he knew the truth about what really happened at her former agency. And when he'd assured her that she'd suffer no such situation here, she'd believed him. It might make her unbelievably naive after her last run-in with her boss, but Brock struck her as a deeply honorable man, and more importantly, someone who kept his word.

"Is everything all right?"

Evan's softly spoken question jarred her from her thoughts. His hand had gone to hers, and he carefully uncurled her fingers that were wound so tightly that the tips were white.

"Do you have a fear of flying?"

She shook her head. "Sorry. I was thinking about something else."

He studied her intently, his gaze stroking her cheeks and then her mouth.

"Seems a shame to waste time on such unpleasant thoughts."

The urge to deny that her thoughts had been unpleasant lasted all of about two seconds. She wrinkled her nose and grinned ruefully.

"Busted."

He chuckled. "I like an honest woman."

It was then she realized that they were already in the air. Wow, she really must have been intensely lost in thought to have missed the takeoff.

"Relax. There'll be plenty of time to discuss business during our stay. Let's begin the trip by enjoying the short flight."

Either she was exceedingly transparent or he'd just anticipated her jumping into things right away. Either way, she was perfectly willing to delay their discussion until she felt a little more on equal footing. Sitting here in such close proximity on his jet, drinking his wine…it was more than a little overwhelming.

His hand remained on hers, his thumb sliding idly over

her knuckles in a soothing pattern. She liked it. She liked it too much.

Survive, Celia. Survive this weekend. Be a professional. After this weekend you'll only have to see him in a business environment.

She swallowed and let calm descend. There was no way she'd screw this opportunity up just because she couldn't get all her girly hormones in check.

The flight went quickly, and oddly, after the first awkward moments, Celia sat back and enjoyed the casual conversation with Evan. William had kept a steady presence to refill their wineglasses and offer a variety of finger foods. By the time they landed at the Airport in the Sky, Celia was limber and completely relaxed. Probably due to the wine.

They were met by a hotel representative and were quickly whisked into a waiting shuttle. It only took a few minutes to arrive at the gorgeous beachfront resort. It was so beautiful, it took her breath away.

The sunset over the water gave the place a decidedly romantic feel, but then they were here for a wedding, so Celia supposed it was only appropriate that romance positively danced on the air.

Evan escorted Celia through the glass doors into the lobby. A bellhop followed behind with a rolling cart that held their luggage.

"Wait right here," Evan murmured. "Take a seat if you like. I'll get our room keys so we can go up."

Before he could go, a feminine voice rent the air.

"Evan! Oh, Evan, you're here!"

Evan stiffened against Celia. He went positively rigid, and Celia could swear she heard him curse under his breath. Celia turned in the direction of the call and saw a regally dressed older woman hurrying across the lobby, her heels tapping delicately on the polished floor.

Behind her, a grim faced older gentleman flanked by a younger woman and a man who looked slightly younger than Evan, walked slower but with no less purpose in Evan's direction.

To her surprise, Evan took her left hand in his and held it close to his side. He fumbled with her fingers even as he looked up with a welcoming smile. It looked completely forced to Celia, but the woman didn't seem put off.

The woman threw her arms around Evan, and still, he didn't let go of Celia's hand. He returned her embrace with his free arm and said, "Hello, Mom. I told you I was coming."

"I know, but after Bettina told me she'd been to see you and when she told me that…"

She broke off and looked curiously at Celia, whose hand was still securely held in Evan's.

Then his mom looked back at Bettina, confusion clear in her eyes.

"But my dear, you told me that Evan wasn't seeing anyone, that he just told me that to ease my concern."

"Did she?" Evan asked in an even tone. He pinned Bettina with a stare that would have had Celia fidgeting.

His mom nudged him impatiently. "Well, introduce us, Evan."

"Yes, do introduce us," Bettina said in a chilly voice.

About the time she felt Evan's grip on her hand tighten and the cool metal slide over her finger, Celia regretted having agreed to come. She tried to look down, wondering what Evan had done to her finger, but he kept his hand over hers. Awkward didn't begin to cover it. She felt as if she'd just entered a minefield.

"Mom. Dad. Bettina. Mitchell." His lips curled when he said the last and Celia zeroed in on the man in question. He had to be Evan's brother. The similarity was striking. "I'd like you to meet—" His entire body tensed and he gripped her hand almost painfully. It was like he was sending her a silent message. "I'd like you to meet my fiancée, Celia Taylor."

Six

Celia froze. There was a horrible buzz in her ears, and she stared in horror at Evan. She hadn't heard him right. What kind of idiotic thing had he just done?

She wasn't sure who was more stunned. Her or his family. Bettina looked as if she just swallowed a lemon. Mitchell looked annoyed, while Evan's father simply frowned. His mom was the only person who actually seemed happy about the bomb.

"Oh, Evan, that's wonderful!"

Celia found herself in the older woman's arms and was hugged so tight that she was in danger of passing out.

"I'm so glad to meet you, my dear."

She held Celia out at arm's length and beamed at her. Then she proceeded to kiss her on both cheeks and if that wasn't enough, she yanked her into another long hug.

This was insane. Evan was insane. His entire family was nuts. She opened her mouth to blast Evan with both barrels and ask him what the hell kind of stunt he was trying to pull when Evan's father put his hand on Evan's shoulder to steer him away from the women.

"Come with me and we'll get you checked in and get your keys. Then you can take Celia up to the room."

Evan looked a little reluctant to leave her. She could well imagine why.

It was then that she remembered her finger. He'd put something on her finger.

She looked down. Holy cow! He'd slipped a huge diamond engagement ring on her finger while he'd held her hand. Fury simmered in her veins. She mentally counted to ten just so she didn't explode on the spot. The bastard had planned this all along. No one carried around a rock like this for the hell of it.

"You two go on ahead and be seated. Order our drinks. Marshall and I will be along in just a moment. I want the chance to speak to Celia for a moment."

Celia regarded Evan's mom warily as she shooed Mitchell and Bettina on toward the hotel restaurant.

When they'd disappeared, only after Bettina had glared enough holes in Celia to rival a hunk of Swiss cheese, Evan's mom seized Celia's hands and squeezed affectionately.

"Oh, my dear, I'm so thrilled to meet you. I can't tell you how fantastic your news is. I was so worried about Evan. He didn't take Bettina's defection very well, but look at you! Even more gorgeous than Bettina. I can see why Evan was so taken with you."

Celia opened her mouth and halted. What on earth could she say? With every word that poured out of the other woman's mouth, the more furious Celia became and the more sickened she was by Evan's deception.

This was some huge soap opera. Things like this didn't happen in real life. Even in really wealthy people's lives, surely.

"By the way, I don't think I introduced myself...well, other than as Evan's mother. I'm Lucy. Please do call me Lucy. Mrs. Reese just sounds so formal and we're going to be family after all."

Celia's heart sank. Lucy obviously was a really wonderful lady and super kindhearted, which only made her angrier that Evan had just lied to her. What the hell had he been thinking?

But then Lucy's other statement came back to her. The

part about Bettina's defection, and suddenly it all made sense.

"Bettina and Evan were involved?" Celia asked.

Lucy colored slightly and looked abashed. "Oh, heavens, I've said too much. I always do have a problem with just prattling on. Do forgive me."

Celia smiled. "It's all right. Truly. It is one of those things women like to know. Men are so thick when it comes to these things, but if any awkwardness can be avoided, I would like to know."

And she could go straight to hell for lying, too. She'd just make sure Evan got there first for his role in this debacle.

"It's all in the past. Rest assured."

"Naturally," Celia said drily.

"Evan and Bettina were engaged. It was a long engagement. The truth of the matter is, I'm just not sure how much of Evan's affections were engaged. Bettina and Mitchell fell in love, and well, it's obvious to anyone that those two were meant for each other. Evan didn't take it well, though, and if I hadn't begged him to come to the wedding, I have no doubt he wouldn't be here."

Lucy smiled and reached out to touch Celia's arm. "Bettina led me to believe that Evan was just going on about being involved because he wasn't over her yet and didn't want to worry me, but I can see that isn't the case. You're even more beautiful than Bettina. I can tell by the way he looks at you that he's besotted. He never looked at Bettina that way."

You are such a sucker, Celia. There should be a law about being so stupid when it came to men. But then she'd spend a lot of time behind bars if that were the case.

She felt Evan's approach. It was hard to miss all that tension. Celia glanced up and met his gaze, and she didn't at all try to disguise her fury. Let him stew. He was damn lucky she liked his mom so much or she would have denounced him in front of the entire hotel lobby.

The poor woman didn't deserve to be humiliated just because her son was a first-rate ass.

Evan regarded her warily even as he turned to his mom. "We'll catch up tomorrow, Mom, okay? Celia and I have had a long day and we'd like to go up and have dinner in the room."

Lucy patted Evan on the cheek and then leaned up on tiptoe to kiss him. "Of course, dear. I'll see you both tomorrow for rehearsal."

She reached back and squeezed Celia's hand. "It was so nice meeting you, Celia."

She walked toward Evan's father and the two went in the direction of the restaurant, leaving Celia and Evan standing in the middle of the lobby.

"We're on the top level," Evan said evenly. He gestured toward the elevator and Celia strode in that direction.

They rode up in silence, the tension so thick Celia felt like the entire elevator would explode before it stopped. It was all she could not to tap her foot in agitation as she waited for the doors to open.

When they finally did, Celia stepped out, glanced down the hall and then back at Evan.

"My key," she said pointedly. "What room am I in?"

Evan sighed and pointed at the end. "We're in the two-bedroom suite on the end."

Her mouth fell open. She reached forward and snatched the key card from his grasp. Then she spun on her heel and stalked down the hall. The hell she'd share a room with him. He could go find other accommodations or he could bunk with his brother. They'd probably have a lot to talk about. Maybe they could compare notes on Bettina.

She jammed the card into the lock, listened for the snick

and then shoved it open. She stepped inside and slammed the door in Evan's face.

Her feet were killing her, she was angry as hell and she was hungry. And she needed to figure out how to get off this damn island.

She kicked off her shoes and then sat on the edge of the couch next to the table with the hotel directory and a telephone. Surely the front desk could make arrangements for her departure.

The sound of the door opening had her on her feet again, and she glared indignantly as Evan walked in and shut the door behind him. He held up another key card in explanation.

He looked tired and resigned.

"Look, I know you're angry."

She held up a hand. "Don't you dare patronize me. You have no idea how furious I am. Angry doesn't even begin to cover it."

He blew out his breath and ran a hand through his hair. He tossed his suit coat onto the arm of the couch.

She pointed to the door with a shaking finger. "Out. I won't share a suite with you. I don't care how many bedrooms it has."

"I need a drink," Evan muttered.

The man wouldn't even fight with her, and by God she wanted a fight.

"You never had any intention of listening to my ideas, did you?"

He stopped on his way over to the liquor cabinet and turned back around to stare at her. He had the audacity to look puzzled.

"I've been such an idiot. I can't believe I fell for this crap. How this was the only time you could fit me in. Blah, blah, blah. How naive does that make me? How stupid does it make me?"

He held up a hand and took a step in her direction. "Celia…"

"Don't Celia me," she whispered furiously. It galled her that she could feel the prick of tears. He would not make her cry. She was through letting men make her cry.

She needed to pull it together and be professional. A really nasty, vivid curse word, one that she'd learned from her brothers burst into her mind. It was certainly appropriate under the circumstances.

Screw professional.

"I have had it with men who manipulate me because of my looks. Here's a clue. I can't help the way I look and it doesn't give you the license to use me or make assumptions about my character. And it damn sure doesn't give you the right to use me to lie to your mother because your fiancée humiliated you by dumping you for your brother. Here's another clue. Crap happens. It happens all the time. Get over it."

Evan's hands closed over her shoulders. She tried to flinch away, but he held tight. There was honest regret in his eyes, but there was also determination. Stubborn determination.

"Sit down, Celia," he ordered in a low voice.

She gaped at him.

"Please."

It was the please that did it. Or maybe it was how tired and resigned he sounded. Or maybe it was the bleak light that entered his eyes. Or maybe she was just a flaming idiot who deserved everything she got for being sucked into this in the first place.

She sank onto the sofa, her entire body trembling as he took a seat beside her.

"I'm sorry," he said. "I don't expect you to believe I didn't do this maliciously or to hurt you. I swear, I didn't."

She cast a sideways glance at him.

He sighed. "Someone really did a number on you, didn't they?"

She turned away, refusing to give him confirmation.

"Celia, look at me."

He waited, and she stared ahead. Still, he waited. Finally, she gave in and turned to look at him.

"I completely and utterly messed this up. I freely admit it. I expected to have time to discuss this with you before we ran into my family."

She struggled to control her temper. He obviously wanted a reasonable discussion when she was feeling anything but reasonable. What she really wanted was to crack his skull on the coffee table and leave, but then she'd be without a room, and if anyone was sleeping in the hallway, it wasn't going to be her.

"First, this has nothing—and I mean nothing—to do with you landing my account. You're going to have to do that on your business and advertising savvy. I'm not putting my entire company in the hands of a woman based on her looks or anything else. Can we at least be clear on that?"

She swallowed. "That's not how it looks to me, Evan. It looks to me like I got played for the fool and that you led me here on the premise of listening to my pitch when you never had any intention of this being about business. Tell me this much, have you already signed with Golden Gate? You owe me that much honesty at least."

Evan gripped a handful of his hair and closed his eyes. "You're pissed. I get it. You have every right to be, but will you please listen to my explanation. If afterward you want me to take a flying leap, I'll be more than happy to accommodate you. You'll never hear from me again."

"I think you know I don't have any other choice," she said helplessly.

"I'll try to make this as short and as concise as possible."

She nodded.

"I didn't have any intention of coming to this damn wedding. I couldn't care less if they live happily ever after and I have even less interest in being here to wish them well along that path to happily ever after.

"Then my mother called and she begged me to come. She was worried that I wasn't over Bettina and that's why I wouldn't come. The woman has a heart of gold, but she obviously knows nothing about me or she'd realize that Bettina was nothing to me the moment she left me for what she perceived to be the better catch."

"Harsh," Celia murmured.

"Is it? I'm only speaking the truth. Bettina was calculating. She hedged her bets and went with Mitchell as soon as he was named my father's successor in the family jewelry business. To her it seemed a more glamorous life. I'd like to be a fly on the wall when she realizes how wrong she is."

Celia's lips curled in amusement. "Not feeling a wee bit vindictive, are you?"

He gave a short laugh. "I may not harbor any love for the woman, and I may not be a bit sorry that she's out of my life, but she is a manipulative cat, and I won't be sorry to see her suffer for the choice she made."

"So your mom doesn't think you're over Bettina. That has what to do with me and this hoax you're perpetuating? Which I really resent by the way because your mom is nice. I feel like pond scum for deceiving her."

"I'm getting there. Just bear with me. When I got off the phone with Mom, I was angry because I let her talk me into going and I said as a last-minute thing that I was bringing someone. I fully intended to look up someone I'd seen casually in the past. Then I remembered that Friday I was supposed to be meeting you and that this meeting was extremely important to me. It seemed logical to combine the two and bring you out with me. I didn't lie about needing to move on this fast. I've wasted weeks listening to pitches. I'm ready to move."

"I'm still seeing a *but* here," she muttered.

"The but occurred when Bettina herself came to see me. She was steamed that I had the audacity to bring someone to her wedding. She felt like it was a poke in the eye at her, and if you can believe, she honestly thinks I'm still pining over her. She basically accused me of being a fraud and of trying to upstage her at her own wedding."

Celia burst out laughing. God, he didn't even see it. How typical a clueless male was he.

"What's so damn funny?" he demanded.

"She accused you of doing exactly what you're doing! The audacity. You crack me up."

He blinked and then looked a little sheepish. "Okay, I get it. I'm an immature, egotistical man. The male ego is obviously a fragile creature. I think we can agree on that. Yes, it occurred to me to get a little of mine back on her by showing up with a gorgeous, stunning woman. Sue me. I even hatched the whole engagement scheme complete with the ring because I figured it was the best way to get them all off my back."

Her shoulders shook and she closed her eyes. The man was nothing if not honest. She had to give him that much.

"Celia, look at me, please."

His entreating tone had her turning once more to stare into those intense green eyes. He looked earnest, and he looked…worried.

"I didn't do any of this to hurt you, I swear. I thought if I just came out and asked you to do me this favor, you'd have never agreed to come with me, even with the promise of listening to your pitch."

"So you lured me here and ambushed me instead," she said drily.

"It didn't go exactly as I'd planned. I'd hoped to have a nice dinner together in our suite and I was going to ask you to do me a personal favor then. I was going to outline the entire charade and ask you to play along. Just for the time we're here. But that all went to hell when we immediately ran into my parents."

His hand crept over hers, and she didn't pull away. She should. She should already be on her way back to San Francisco, and she should be calling Brock to tell him that there was no way in hell she was delivering Evan Reese on a platter to Maddox Communications.

She pressed her lips together and tried to collect her scattered thoughts. "So you want me to pretend to be your fiancée." She lifted her hand to angle the huge diamond in the light. "Complete with a really gorgeous ring. What happens after the wedding?"

Evan shrugged. "We break up quietly later. They'll never know the difference. We don't see each other that often. One day Mom will call and I'll say 'oh, by the way, Celia and I broke things off.' And that will be that."

She shook her head. "All of this because you couldn't stand the thought of your fiancée thinking you weren't over her?"

Evan scowled. "It's not that simple. There are other factors. Besides, we've already established the fact that I'm an egotistical, immature male. We don't have to go back into that territory."

"Poor baby." She patted his arm and then laughed at his disgruntled look. "I can't believe I'm even considering this."

His eyes glinted predatorily. "But you are."

"Yes, dammit, I am. I'm a sucker for immature, egotistical males. But we need to establish a few ground rules."

"Of course," he said solemnly.

"My reputation is everything to me, Evan," she said quietly. "I won't have any notion of impropriety attached to this account. I won't have it bandied around that I got the account because I slept with you."

Something that looked an awful lot like lust gleamed in his eyes a second before he blinked and adopted a more serious expression.

"This favor is separate. If I don't like your ideas, you'll go home without my business. It's that simple. Agreeing to be my fake fiancée doesn't buy you anything but my gratitude. It won't land you Reese Enterprises. Are we clear on that?"

"Crystal," she said. "Tell me something, Evan. If I refuse to play the part of your lover, are you still going to hear my pitch? Are you even going to consider Maddox?"

"Well, I do have a fragile ego, remember?"

"Will you be serious?"

A grin worked at the corners of her mouth. She should be mad as hell at this man, not entertained by his self-effacing wit. And she definitely shouldn't be attracted to his boyish charm or his straightforward handling of this entire ridiculous affair.

"I tell you what, Celia. The plan was always to have a quiet dinner in tonight where I could explain my plan and beg you to go along. Then tomorrow morning we were going to have our business meeting, again, in the privacy of our hotel suite. Afterward we would perpetuate my silly hoax on my brother and his grasping, manipulative bride-to-be. See? Completely separate."

"You are completely irreverent, and I'm disgusted that I like it so much."

He smiled, and his eyes twinkled with amusement. "You're as diabolical as I am, face it."

"I could have used some of your evilness in the past.

That's for sure. I'm a little envious of how you don't mind poking your finger in the eyes of those who have screwed you over. I need to learn how to do that."

He cocked his head to the side. "What happened to you, Celia?"

She flushed and turned away. "It's nothing. Definitely in the past and that's where I want it to stay."

"Okay. Fair enough. But I hope one day you'll tell me."

"We don't have that kind of relationship," she said lightly.

"No," he murmured. "We don't. Not yet."

Her gaze lifted but his expression didn't betray his thoughts. She swallowed the knot in her throat and hoped she wasn't making a huge, huge mistake. So much could go wrong with this.

"You're so worried about the position I've placed you in," he said. "But the truth is, if I don't like your ideas tomorrow morning, what's to say that you don't leave me to face the festivities on my own? I'd say that gives you all the power and none to me."

"Or you could just say you like my ideas to keep me on the line long enough to get through the wedding," she pointed out. "Nothing to say that you don't dump me the minute we get back to San Francisco."

He nodded. "True. All of it is true. Looks like we both have some trusting to do."

She looked down at her hand that was still underneath his. His thumb pressed into her palm, and his fingers lay still over hers, but the warmth of his touch spread up her entire arm and into her chest.

She liked this man. Genuinely liked him, stupid ambush aside. He hadn't sugarcoated any of it. And above all else, she liked honesty. He hadn't shied away from how the entire situation made him look. It certainly didn't make him appear very noble, but she couldn't get beyond thinking he was just that. Noble and honest.

The ring on her finger sparkled and glinted in the light. For just one moment, she allowed herself to imagine what it would be like if it were all real. Two seconds later she mentally slapped herself silly and told herself to get over her foolishness.

She had a job to do. She had to impress this man with her brains and her creativity, her drive and her determination. She could do all that. And if it meant she had to go beyond the call of duty to do a personal favor for him, then she needed to suck it up and just get the job done. Too many people were counting on her.

It was silly. She felt like an idiot and she was sure Evan didn't feel any better, but it wasn't up to her to question his motives. For whatever reason, he didn't want his brother and his fiancée to see him bleed. She could understand that. She would have died rather than let her old boss and his scheming wife know how much they'd destroyed her.

"All right, Evan. I'll do it."

Triumph mixed with relief flared to life in his eyes.

"Thank you for not bashing my skull in and leaving, but more than that, thank you for not reacting in front of my family. It was more than I deserved given how I sprang it on you. I swear, that was not the way I wanted to approach you with my proposition."

"If we're done with all that, can we eat? I'm starving. You can tell me all I need to know about your family and also tell me how it was we met and when you proposed, but not until I get something to eat."

He leaned forward, caught her jaw in his hand and turned her toward him. Their lips were so close that his breath blew warm over her mouth. She swallowed nervously, wondering if he would kiss her. And then she wondered if she'd let him. Or if she would kiss him instead.

"Thank you," he murmured.

Slowly, he withdrew, and to her chagrin, disappointment washed over her.

Seven

Evan watched as Celia sat sideways on the couch, her back against the arm and her knees doubled in front of her. She looked comfortable and completely relaxed, which was more than he could have hoped for given how stupidly he'd sprung the whole engagement thing on her.

After her initial fury, though, she'd calmed down and had taken it well. Damn, but he liked this woman. Oh, he was definitely attracted to her sexually, but beyond that, he genuinely liked spending time with her.

If he was smart, he'd take that as a huge warning sign to stay away and not become involved, but he'd never claimed brilliance.

She'd changed into nothing more glamorous than a pair of sweatpants and a San Francisco Tide jersey. Odd, but she hadn't struck him as a baseball fan.

Her shoes had long since been shed, and her toenails, painted a delicate shade of pink, teased him. Hell, he was even attracted to her feet. Small and dainty.

He was officially losing his mind. Never before had he lusted after a woman's feet.

She forked another bite into her mouth then sighed and made a low sound of agony before putting her plate down on the coffee table.

"That was fabulous. I've eaten so much that I won't fit into that sparkly dress I brought for the wedding."

That statement brought a whole host of splendid ideas to

mind. Namely that they could both skip the wedding and stay in bed where clothing was entirely optional.

He shifted in his seat and wondered for the sixth time why he was so bent on torturing himself.

"So tell me something, Evan," she said as she leaned farther into the sofa cushions. Her eyelids lowered and she tucked those pink toes underneath a throw pillow. "What made you walk away from your family's business and start your own in a field that was so different from the jewelry trade?"

It didn't surprise him that she knew so much about his background. She would have researched him tirelessly. Still, he debated how much to tell her.

Their gazes locked, and he saw only simple curiosity. No ulterior motive, just interest.

"There were several reasons," he finally said. "Emotion has no place in business and yet I find myself making emotional decisions."

Her eyebrows rose. "I'm surprised you'd admit that. Doesn't jive with your big, bad, ruthless businessman persona."

He smiled ruefully. "Okay, so part of it was emotion based. I didn't agree with my father's style of management. The fact is his company is in trouble. I saw it coming years ago and he was in flat denial. He saw no reason to change the way he ran things since it had worked for decades before.

"The other reason was I don't exactly get along that well with him and Mitchell."

"You don't say," she said drily.

He chuckled. "Yeah, I know, hard to believe. Mitchell... there are lots of more appropriate words for him, but I'll go with the fact that he's a lazy, unmotivated brown noser. All his life, because he was the baby, he's never had to actually work for anything. He's been handed everything since he was a child. As a result, his sense of entitlement is huge. I would work for something and he would want what I had worked for. Dad would give it to him."

"Ah, I think I'm beginning to understand the fiancée thing more now."

He nodded. "Yes, I don't harbor any illusion that Mitchell and Bettina are some great love match. I had Bettina, so Mitchell decided he wanted her. Bettina saw Mitchell's appointment to CEO as her ride into a life of glamour."

"And were you and Bettina? A love match, I mean?" she asked gently.

He pursed his lips and blew out a long breath. "This is where I look like the jerk."

Celia chuckled. "Jerk? You? Surely you jest."

"All right, don't rub it in," he grumbled. "I've admitted my shortcomings."

"Do continue. I'm dying to hear all about what a toad you are."

Her eyes sparkled with mischief and amusement. He'd never wanted to kiss her more than he did right now. Instead he found himself telling her stuff he'd never tell a woman he planned to take to bed.

"Bettina didn't pose a challenge. That sounds bad but when I met her, I was devoting all my time to making my business a success. It was exciting and exhilarating. I exceeded even my wildest expectations. Everything was falling into place at the speed of light. All that was missing in my mind to complete the image of perfection I had built up was a wife and a family. Perfect house in the suburbs. I'd come home after a hectic day and she'd have dinner waiting. The kids would all be bathed and well behaved. Even the dog would be the epitome of good behavior. I wanted—still want—a woman who'll put me first."

Celia snorted, covered her mouth and then dissolved into hoots of laughter.

He regarded her dubiously. "I do believe you're mocking me."

"Mocking you?" She wheezed between words and tears gathered in the corners of her eyes. "Oh my, Evan. You do dream big, don't you?"

"Well, it was a good fantasy while it lasted," he grumbled. "I looked around and there was Bettina. I didn't have time to figure out what my ideal woman was. I wanted my perfect life then and I didn't want to wait. So I asked her to marry me, she said yes, I gave her a ring and that was that."

"And yet here you are. With me. The fake fiancée."

He scowled ferociously at her only for her to dissolve into laughter again.

"Okay, so what happened? Other than Mitchell stepping in and being an overindulged twit."

He liked this woman. She was good for his ego even when she was tearing it down.

"Bettina wanted to set an immediate date. She had a grand wedding planned. Even had the honeymoon destination picked out. She littered my office with brochures. Hell, she even had our children's names picked out."

"I would have thought given your fantasy that you would have eaten that up with a spoon," she pointed out.

"Yeah, so did I. Only I found myself backing off. I kept making excuses to extend the engagement. I was busy. This deal had to take priority. That deal needed immediate attention. Before I knew it, we had been engaged a year with a wedding scheduled another year beyond that. And moreover I was content with that."

"Did you never love her?" Celia asked quietly.

"No. No, I didn't. Which is why I can't really blame her for wanting out. Our marriage would have been a disaster just as soon as I figured out the reality didn't live up to the fantasy I'd created in my mind. I just didn't think she'd dump me for Mitchell or that Mitchell would have been poaching on my territory."

Celia winced. "Yeah, I can understand that."

"I found them in bed, you know. How clichéd is that? The sad thing is, when I found them together in my bed, I just laughed, because to me it was just the next step in an already farcical relationship. I tossed them out of my apartment and washed my hands of them both."

Celia's expression grew thoughtful. "Hmm, so you don't necessarily object to the fact that she found someone else. Or that she cheated on you. Just who she indulged herself with."

Evan nodded and rubbed the back of his neck to ease some of the tension and fatigue. Just talking about it raised his ire all over again.

"Yeah, it's stupid I know. I mean, she could have cheated on me with my business partner, or my vice president or, hell, even my driver. I wouldn't have cared. I might have even given the man a raise. But my brother. My spoiled, overindulged brother. No, that was the one thing I couldn't forgive."

"Well, if their relationship is based on all you say, then I'd imagine they'll suffer enough in the long run without you wishing them ill."

He regarded her for a long moment. "You're not going to lecture me about harboring childish grudges?"

She smiled, and those gorgeous green eyes cut right through him. She took his breath away until he was helpless to do anything but stare back.

"Nope. Not a word. Considering I have my own grudges and I don't plan on forgetting them in this lifetime, I could hardly chastise you for the same."

"Oh, do tell. You sound so…vicious. I like it," he teased.

Her expression grew serious. Pain flickered in her eyes, and she turned away, her mouth drawn into a tight line. He was immediately sorry that the light mood had dissolved. As much as he wanted to know her secrets, he wanted to see her laughing and smiling even more.

To cover the sudden heaviness in the air, he got up to pour a glass of wine. Without a word, he offered one to her, and she took it, gratitude easing some of the tightness around her eyes.

He wanted to touch her so badly. Wanted to ease the strain and the unhappy tilt to her lips. He wanted to kiss her plump mouth until he owned her very breath.

He forced himself to return to his chair. The remains of their dinner was scattered across the coffee table. Some had fallen to the floor, but he wasn't inclined to clean it up. They sat there sipping their wine as evening fell all around them.

Finally he could remain silent no more.

He leaned forward to set his glass on the table. For a moment he looked down at his hands and imagined her flesh beneath his fingertips. Then he glanced back up to see her studying him with the same keen interest flashing in her eyes. She wasn't immune. He wasn't the only one who felt the magnetic pull between them.

"What are we going to do, Celia?" he murmured.

He saw her swallow nervously. She hadn't misunderstood, but neither did she respond.

"I want you so damn much I hurt. I've hurt for weeks. Every time I look at you, I get so many knots that I can't function. I've thought of all the ways I can explain to you that our business relationship has nothing to do with the desire I feel for you. But the simple truth is I don't give a damn. I want you in my bed, and I don't care what has to be done to make that happen."

Her eyes went wide and frightened. He hated that. He didn't want her to be afraid of him.

"You feel it, too. Don't deny me that much."

Slowly she nodded. Her fingers went to her forehead and she dug them into her hair. Still, he could see them shaking, and she swallowed again, her slim neck working with the effort.

"Please," she whispered. "I can't do this, Evan. It's the one thing I can't do. Don't ask it of me. If you want me to admit it, fine. I want you. More than I've ever wanted another man."

Savage satisfaction gripped him. Didn't just grip him but lunged for him and wrapped a hand around his throat and his groin. His entire body reacted to that simple statement. She wanted him more than she'd ever wanted anyone else.

She turned on the couch until she faced forward and her feet met the floor. She looked in turns miserable and scared. Her eyes closed in what looked to him like self-condemnation. He swore, startling her with the force of his curses.

"Whatever you're thinking, I don't like it," he said flatly. "I have no idea what the hell kind of blame you're placing on yourself, but I can guarantee that you didn't use your feminine wiles to seduce me into signing with your agency. I wanted you from the first moment I saw you. Want to know when that was, Celia? Go ahead, ask me."

He stared at her in blatant challenge, waiting, wanting her to take it up.

Her eyes went wide with shock, and her face was pale and drawn. "W-when?"

"At the Sutherlands' reception. You were there with one of your clients. Copeland, if I remember correctly. The grocery-store giant."

Her mouth fell open. "But you were still with Rencom."

He nodded. "Precisely. I looked across the room, and you took my breath away. Want to know another of my sins, Celia? I was still engaged to Bettina. It was a week before I found her in bed with Mitchell. I didn't care. I wanted you so much. Now tell me how big of a bastard that makes me. Try to tell me this has anything to do with your pitch."

In the course of their conversation, he'd moved to the couch. He moved closer still, stalking her like prey. Her scent lured him, and he inhaled the delicate, feminine smell that he'd come to associate with only her.

Her eyes were flush with awareness and caution. There was confusion in her deep green pools, but something else, too. Desire. Matching desire. She wanted him. Maybe as much as he wanted her. It didn't matter because he would have her.

"Want to know something else?" he murmured. "I almost didn't consider Maddox for the account. Want to know why? Because I didn't want it to interfere with my pursuit of you."

He was close now. So close he could feel every little puff of breath that came from her lips. He could see the tiny little nervous swallows that worked her throat up and down. And her mouth. Her luscious, sweet mouth. He wanted to taste it, devour it like candy.

"W-what changed your mind?" she whispered.

"I'm perfectly capable of separating business from pleasure," he said evenly.

"Evan, we can't."

She put her hand on his chest. Big mistake. A current of electricity singed him. They both jumped, but before she could withdraw, he caught her fingers and trapped her hand between his and his chest.

"Just one kiss, Celia. Just one. I have to kiss you. It's all I'll demand for now. I can wait for more until we have this account settled."

Without waiting for her consent, he swept his mouth over hers. Finally. Her sweetness exploded onto his tongue the moment he licked over her lips. Her mouth parted in a gasp, and he took full advantage, delving deep into her moist heat.

She made the sweetest sounds. He swallowed them up as he devoured every inch of her mouth. He was transfixed by her full bottom lip. He nipped lightly at it, teasing it to fullness and then he sucked it between his teeth.

Her tongue stroked tentatively over his, just light brushes with the tip and then she grew bolder, taking a more active part in the kiss.

His hands delved into her hair. He loved her hair. Long and glorious, the color like a russet sunset over the desert. The temptation was too great. He'd fantasized about it for too long.

He fumbled with the clip and released its hold on her hair. It tumbled down her back, over his hands like a wave. He gathered the strands between his fingers, mesmerized by their silky smoothness.

He drank deeply, not wanting the moment to end. He could spend hours kissing her, but he wanted more. He wanted to work his mouth down the curve of her jaw to her neck. He wanted to peel every layer of clothing from her body and then run his tongue over her soft skin.

He wondered what her breasts would feel like in his hands and what her nipples would taste like, how they'd feel as he sucked them into his mouth.

Oh, yes, he'd spent a lot of time wondering about her breasts. She never wore clothing that could be deemed too provocative. She was fashionable, yes, but he secretly wished she'd wear something a little more revealing. It was killing him not to get a hint of her full, ripe breasts.

Soon. Soon, he'd unwrap all of her. He'd possess her. She'd be his.

He needed air and he broke away only long enough to pull oxygen into his starving lungs. She gasped along with him, and then he started at the corner of her mouth and licked and kissed his way across to the other corner.

Her small hands slid up his chest. It was like a heating element sliding over his skin. She left a blazing trail of fierce need in her wake. His entire body came alive, and all she'd done was touch him. Innocently.

They wound up around his neck and then her fingertips just delved into the hair at his nape. He shuddered, and it was all he could do to retain his tight hold on his control.

His body screamed at him to haul her over his shoulder and drag her caveman-style to the bedroom. He'd rip off her clothes and spend the night taking her over and over until they both succumbed to exhaustion.

His mind yelled at him to be careful. To take it slow. Not to push her so far away that she never returned.

It was that fear of driving her away permanently that finally pulled him back from the brink of insanity.

With great reluctance, he pulled back. His hands were still tangled up in her hair, and he carefully extricated them from the heavy coil that lay over her shoulders.

Her eyes were cloudy, a gorgeous mix of confusion and desire that had him wanting to throw caution to the wind and continue his seduction.

"That," he whispered, "is what I've been wanting to do ever since I saw you across a crowded room six months ago. Now you tell me this has anything to do with Maddox Communications and Reese Enterprises."

Her hand fluttered to her mouth and she stared at him with shocked awareness.

"Oh, God, Evan. What are we going to do?"

He smiled gently and slowly pulled her hand away from her swollen lips.

"What we're going to do is get your pitch out of the way tomorrow morning. Whatever happens afterward, we take it as it comes."

Eight

There was no need for Celia to set her alarm. She never went to sleep. She lay in bed, staring at the ceiling, her senses completely shattered by something as simple as a kiss.

No. That kiss could never ever be called simple.

She'd thought to go over her pitch. Mentally replay everything she wanted to say until it flowed seamlessly through her mind. But all she'd been able to do was lay there and wonder how she was going to manage to keep things with Evan on a strictly professional level.

He kissed like a dream.

He'd make love like a dream.

And the sick thing was she'd never find out.

She rolled over and buried her face in her pillow.

Celia, Celia.

The admonishment burned like acid on her tongue. She was walking a very tight, very dangerous line. It was bad enough that she was here with Evan. Sharing a suite with Evan. Her groan was swallowed up by the pillow.

The least she could have done was insisted on a separate room, but that wouldn't have gone far in convincing his family that they were happily engaged.

Friendship. Okay, she could handle a friendship with Evan. She liked him. He asked her to consider this a personal favor. As a friend. And she'd forget the kiss. Forget that he had made his intention to make love to her abundantly clear.

All she had to do was get through her presentation, go to a rehearsal dinner, wedding and reception with Evan— as his fiancée—and then she could go home and put him firmly back in his neat, tidy little corner.

She struggled out of bed, knowing it would take her the better part of an hour to erase the look of someone who hadn't slept. Evan had ordered room service to be brought up at eight, and she wanted plenty of time to go over her notes again.

She purposely toned down her looks, choosing subtle makeup. She did nothing to highlight her eyes, which were her best feature. And she pulled her hair back into a tight knot and used hairspray to keep the wispy tendrils from escaping. She wanted no distractions. No sizzling looks. No temptation to do something utterly stupid.

To her immense relief, when she walked out of her bedroom, Evan was in total business mode. He didn't stare at her like he was set to devour her. He gave her a cursory glance and motioned for her to sit across from him at the dining table where breakfast had already been served.

"We can eat and talk, or we can eat and then talk. Strictly up to you," he said when she took her seat.

"We can eat and talk," she said. "I'm not using props or anything, and I planned it to be more conversational than a formal presentation."

He nodded approvingly. "Great. Let's dig in and get started then."

There was a moment of transition where they ate in silence before Celia shut off everything but the task at hand. This was her career and she knew she was damn good at it. She hadn't gotten to where she was and survived the pitfalls without the ability to put her game face on in the face of adversity.

"I studied your last ad campaign, and I believe you're missing a huge segment of your target audience."

He blinked, set his fork down and stared across at her. "Okay, you have my attention."

"Perhaps I should put it another way. I think you're not targeting the right audience. You're missing a huge opportunity."

She paused for effect and then segued into her spiel.

"Right now you appeal to the sports crowd. The guy who jogs. The woman who goes to the gym. The person who cares about staying in shape. You're all about functionality. The kids who play sports. The guys who play racquetball at the club. The casual basketball game on the weekends."

Evan nodded.

"Then there are the people, like me, who are allergic to physical activity."

He snorted and sent an appraising look over her body.

She ignored him and continued on.

"These are the people who watch sports. They're tuned in to every game. The players. The teams. They run the gambit from the fanatic to the casual observer. They're the people who will buy your sportswear not because they're going to worry over the functionality. They don't care. They want to look cool. They want to immerse themselves in the aura of the sports world. You're a brand, a label. It's a status symbol."

Her excitement mounted with every word. He was listening intently. She had him.

"So you do dual marketing. You go after the die-hard fitness enthusiast with the sweaty workout commercials. The driven athlete who's going to be the best and wearing your brand the entire time."

Again she paused to gauge his reaction, and he was leaning forward, his brow creased in concentration.

"Then you go after the men and the women and the kids who want your clothing and your shoes because they look good. Because they make them feel athletic without ever lifting a finger. You show them someone looking cool and sophisticated in your clothing. You show them it's hip to have Reese Wear. They can be average, everyday Joes and still know what it feels like to be a star."

Then she went for the kill shot. Her excitement mounted because she knew he was interested. This had nothing to do with personal attraction. He was all business right now and his eyes gleamed with enthusiasm.

"And the person you show to both of these groups, the man you have doing the sweaty, driven shoots and the cool, suave commercials is Noah Hart."

Evan's eyes widened a fraction, and then he sat back in his seat. "Wait a minute."

She waited, trying valiantly to hide her smug grin. This would be the fun part.

"You're telling me you can get me Noah Hart?" He didn't even wait for her to reply. "Companies have been after Noah Hart ever since he entered the major leagues."

"Before," she said airily. "They wanted him out of college."

"Whatever. The point is, the man has never agreed to an endorsement deal. What makes you think you can change his mind?"

"And if I told you he's willing to talk to you?"

"No way," Evan breathed.

"It'll cost you."

"Hell, it would be worth it!" His eyes narrowed again. "He'll talk to me. You've already been in contact with him?"

"I might have mentioned the possibility of you doing a new ad campaign."

"And he's interested?"

"He'll talk to you. I provided him research, which means you passed the first round of scrutiny with him.

He's a hard guy. You land him and it'll be huge. Not only will you have a kick-ass ad campaign, but you'll also be the guy who signed Noah Hart."

"I'd want exclusivity," Evan said quickly.

"You'd have to be prepared to pay for that privilege," Celia pointed out. She wasn't about to tell Evan that exclusivity or not, the chances of Noah agreeing to do another deal with someone else were slim to none. The man simply wasn't motivated by money.

"Okay, let's forget Noah Hart for the moment. I like your ideas, Celia. I mean, the average Joe has never escaped my notice, but you're right. I've never gone after him in marketing. My commercials are always about the drive to succeed. I talk to the athlete in all of us."

"Which I've just pointed out doesn't exist in everyone," she said drily.

"Yes, you're right. Completely. The junior-high kid trying to look cool. Huge market there that I've yet to tap."

"Most of my ideas are about how to structure television commercials, Internet advertising and print media to target all segments of the population from the die-hard sports and fitness enthusiast to Suzy Homemaker who just wants a comfortable pair of tennis shoes. We'd speak separately to teens, young adults all the way up to the retired folks."

Evan nodded. "I'm interested. Definitely interested. When can you have a presentation put together for me? As I said before, I'm ready to move on this. I don't mind taking a little extra time if I can be guaranteed better results."

"You tell me when you can meet with us at Maddox and I'll arrange it," she said evenly.

"And Noah Hart?"

"I'll arrange it as soon as we get back."

"Then I'd say you've got your pitch appointment, Celia. I'm very impressed with what you've had to say. If your presentation delivers on the promise of your ideas, it's something my company will be very excited about."

Though she had every confidence in her ability to win him over, his enthusiasm gave her a wicked thrill. She was forced to play it cool and smile politely as she thanked him, but on the inside she was doing an insane victory dance.

She had phone calls to make. Brock would need to know so they could start preparing. They'd want to do mock-ups of the advertising and have it prominently displayed on the television monitors in the Maddox reception area. On the day she'd give Evan her presentation, Maddox Communications would be all about Reese Enterprises. No one else would exist in the timeframe Evan was present in their offices.

"You have to tell me how you managed to get Noah Hart to agree to talk to me," Evan said as he pushed his plate aside.

A small smile flirted at the edges of her mouth and she suppressed the urge to grin broadly.

"I can't reveal all my secrets."

"You pull this off and you'll be legendary," Evan said. "The man has never so much as been tempted to take a deal."

Okay, now she felt a little like a fraud. Legendary indeed. While she did love having an ace up her sleeve, she felt a little squeamish over Evan's praise. Noah Hart was her big brother, and the truth was, there wasn't much he wouldn't do for his little sister. Never mind that she'd never asked him for any such favor before. She was this time, and it was the only reason Noah was contemplating breaking his long-held policy.

"Don't fawn yet," she murmured. "He might prove to be too expensive for you."

Evan's eyes glinted with a predatory gleam. He had the look of a man sure of himself and all things.

"I've not found many things in life that proved to be too expensive. I may not always want to pay the price, but rarely have I found them out of my range."

She smiled. "I sensed that about you, which is why I thought you might be the one Noah would come to terms with. I think the two of you are probably a lot alike."

Evan cocked his head to the side. "Just how well do you know him?"

Her lips lifted again, but she didn't answer. Evan's BlackBerry rang and provided much needed distraction. She wasn't ready to tell Evan about her relationship with Noah. Not yet.

She tuned into Evan's conversation when he said her name. He was obviously talking to his mom.

"We'll be there this afternoon. Four o'clock. Yes, I know. I won't miss it. Dinner afterward. Celia and I are having lunch together down by the marina. We'll meet you back at the hotel in time for rehearsal. You have my word."

He hung up and let out a sigh as he tucked the phone back into his pocket.

"The woman is convinced I'll flake on the wedding. I wonder how on earth she got that idea?"

It was said so innocently that Celia burst into laughter. Evan joined her and business was effectively put back out of the way once more.

Nine

The nice lunch by the harbor never happened. As Evan and Celia were leaving the hotel, they ran into Evan's parents and Mitchell and Bettina.

Lucy was thrilled, since they were on their way to lunch, as well, and she suggested they eat together before they gathered on the terrace for the very informal rehearsal.

It amused Celia that there would even be an actual rehearsal of the ceremony since it wasn't a big affair and the bride and groom only had two attendants each. Still, it was evidently important to keep up appearances because they were going all out with a full-blown rehearsal and a dinner and party afterward.

Bettina acted less than thrilled that Celia and Evan would be joining them for lunch. Mitchell was visibly uncomfortable. When they were seated, as luck would have it, Evan and Celia were placed across the table from Bettina and Mitchell while Lucy and Marshall sat on the ends.

As a result, Celia was treated to Bettina's malevolent stare. The woman wasn't even subtle about it. She picked Celia apart like a bug under a microscope.

Evan reached for her hand under the table and gave her a squeeze. She couldn't figure out if it was a gesture of support, sympathy or a thank-you.

She turned and gave him a smile. For a long moment their gazes locked and he smiled back.

"Tell me, Celia, what is it that you do? Evan tells me

you live in San Francisco. Will you be moving once you and Evan are married?"

Celia turned to Lucy in surprise. The questions were natural for a mother to ask, but Celia hadn't been prepared for them. Who was she kidding? She hadn't been prepared for any of this.

"Celia is a crack advertising executive," Evan smoothly inserted. "We haven't discussed where we'll live after we're married. Her career is very important to her. I'd never expect her to give it up."

Oh, the man was good. If she was getting married, she'd want the guy she was marrying to say exactly what Evan had said, and she'd want him to mean every word.

Bettina sniffed. "But don't you feel a woman's place is at home with the children? You do plan on having children don't you?"

Celia frowned as she stared at the other woman. Was she for real? Granted she was young. Celia guessed she was in her early twenties. What the hell had Evan been thinking when he'd hooked up with her in the first place? She was practically an infant and Evan had to be pushing forty.

"I don't see that it's any of your concern whether I want children or not and as for where my place is, it's wherever I'm the happiest," Celia said. "I fail to see how I could possibly be the best wife and mother by staying at home and being miserable."

Bettina looked genuinely confused. "I feel it's important for a woman not to overshadow her husband. A husband's job is to provide for his family. I'd never take that away from him."

Celia snorted. "You keep telling yourself that, honey. Call me up when your provider husband has decided he no longer wants that job and is going to leave you and the children to go find himself. Then tell me how important it was for you to depend solely on him for your support, and then tell me how easy it is to go find a job making enough money to support yourself and your children when the sole job experience on your resume is changing diapers and cooking dinner."

Evan choked on his laughter while Lucy's eyes widened in shock. Mitchell looked a little green while Bettina's mouth hung open. Marshall cleared his throat and actually looked at Celia with something akin to respect.

"Well said, young lady. A woman should never put the welfare of herself and her children solely in her husband's hands no matter how solid the relationship."

"Marshall!"

Lucy sounded positively scandalized.

Evan sat back and looked at his dad. "You see why I'm so determined to marry her. If my company ever goes bankrupt, I can stay at home and let her support me."

The two men burst into laughter and Evan squeezed her hand harder.

"Have you two set a date yet?" Mitchell asked, entering the conversation for the first time.

He'd been strangely silent, and he'd studied her and Evan until Celia squirmed under his scrutiny.

Not wanting Evan to do all the talking, even if this was his charade and not hers, she smiled and looked back at Mitchell.

"He's only just convinced me to marry him. I did make him wait, and he had to ask me several times."

Evan squeezed again only this time it was a definite retaliation squeeze. She grinned and plunged ahead.

"I finally put him out of his misery and said yes. He wants a short engagement." Some little evil imp made her poke Bettina a little with that statement since Evan had kept prolonging their engagement. "He wanted to elope to Las Vegas, but I want to take our time and really get to know each other before we tie the knot."

Evan made a strangled noise and promptly took a long drink of his wine. Celia kept a perfectly straight face as she took in the reactions of Evan's family.

Lucy looked wary. Bettina looked murderous. Mitchell had a strange look that could only be interpreted as a cross between regret and sadness while Marshall nodded approvingly. He reached over to slap his son on the back.

"You've got yourself a winner here, son. I heartily approve. This one will keep you on your toes well into your old age. I like her."

Greaaat. She had the approval of her fake father-in-law to be. She looked over at Evan as guilt swamped her. She'd gotten carried away and hadn't been able to resist the opportunity to needle Evan a bit. Though he deserved it, she still felt bad about carrying things so far.

To her surprise, he was staring thoughtfully at her, his eyes warm with something she was afraid to analyze.

"I absolutely agree," Evan murmured. "I'm a very lucky man."

Evan kept a possessive arm wrapped around Celia's waist as they navigated the small field of people in the ballroom where everyone had gathered after the rehearsal dinner.

A band played, and already several couples were dancing, his mom and dad included.

He knew the closeness between him and Celia was all for show, but the primitive part of him recognized his desire to publicly brand her as his woman. She'd probably knee him right in the groin if she had any inkling what his thoughts were. The image made him wince and chuckle all at the same time.

Every time he looked at Bettina, he was gripped by such gratitude and relief that it staggered him. How close he'd come to an unmitigated disaster.

All the things he had thought he wanted were ludicrous in hindsight. A woman like Bettina would never hold his attention for long. She didn't challenge him.

He wanted someone intelligent, as driven as he was, someone he could consider a partner.

Someone like Celia.

His lips tightened. Thanks to his decision to go with Maddox—he hadn't told Celia yet—a relationship between them was impossible. Not that he'd give a rat's ass that she worked for him indirectly, but Celia would never agree.

"If you hold me any tighter, someone's going to call the police on us," Celia murmured.

He loosened his hold on her waist and uttered a low apology.

"Let's dance," she suggested. "You're way too tense. No one's ever going to believe we're newly engaged and head over heels in loooove with you scowling like that."

"You're right. Sorry. Got distracted."

"I'll try not to take that personally," she teased.

He relaxed immediately and let her pull him onto the dance floor. The music was slow and seductive and gave him the perfect opportunity to do what he'd been wanting to do all damn day. Hold her flush against his body so he could feel every one of her soft, delectable curves.

They fit perfectly and he tucked her as close as she would go. His cheek rested against her temple as he slowly whirled her around the floor. Her hips swayed, brushing her belly across his groin. He let one hand trail down her spine and over the curve of one hip.

She tensed a moment, and he wondered if she'd tell him to back off but then she relaxed with a sigh and melted into his arms once more.

"You were fantastic at lunch today," he said against her ear. "I never thought my father would become such a fan. He's typically a stodgy, conservative chauvinist."

Her shoulders shook with laughter. "He'd fit in quite well with my family then. My father and brothers think my sole ambition in life should be to look pretty and let them take care of me."

"I'm going to admit something," he said gravely.

She turned her face up, her eyes sparkling with amusement. "Oh, do tell. Is this where you divulge your deepest, darkest secrets?"

"You could try to express an appropriate amount of appreciation for my confiding in you," he huffed.

"Very well. Let me just bat my eyelashes in adoration, but be quick or I'll mess up my mascara."

He shook his head as helpless laughter escaped. "What I was going to admit was that while I truly appreciate and agree with everything you had to say, there is a caveman lurking underneath my civilized exterior. I can see why your family wants to protect and take care of you. I think if you were mine, I'd feel much the same way."

Her lips parted, and she stared at him with the oddest expression. There was no anger or condemnation. Interest and something else gleamed in her emerald eyes.

"And sometimes I think if you were mine, I just might let you," she said huskily.

His entire body tightened. His hand raced up her spine and he curled his fingers gently at her nape. Their eyes were locked together and all he had to do was lean down. Just a bit. He could taste her already.

His head lowered. Her eyes narrowed to slits and she let out a breathy, feminine sigh of anticipation.

"Evan, you've monopolized her long enough."

His father's voice boomed in his ears and Evan jumped, sending Celia away from him for a brief moment.

Marshall stood there expectantly. "Going to let me cut in?"

Evan slipped Celia's hand into his father's. "Of course. Just don't keep her for long."

Marshall chuckled as he spirited Celia away. "One dance won't kill you, son."

Evan watched his dad whirl Celia across the floor. In a word, she was magnificent. She laughed at something he said and her smile lit up the entire room. She sparkled.

"Quite a woman," Mitchell drawled.

Evan stiffened and turned to see his brother standing there, drink in hand.

"Where's the bride-to-be?" Evan asked. "Didn't figure she'd let you out of her sight until the vows are spoken."

Mitchell shrugged. "She's over with Mom, talking about the honeymoon arrangements." He looked again at Celia and their father. "You're marrying her for real?"

"Is there some reason I shouldn't?" Evan asked mildly.

"Doesn't seem your type."

Evan regarded his brother with curiosity. "And what is my type?"

"Someone like Bettina. You seemed pretty hung up on her."

"I think it's safe to say I'm not hung up on Bettina."

"I can see why you're attracted to her," Mitchell said.

"Who?" Evan demanded sharply.

"Celia."

Both men stared across the room to where Celia danced with Marshall.

"She's a beautiful woman. I bet she's awesome in bed."

Evan rounded furiously on his brother. "You shut the hell up. Don't even breathe her name again. You got it?"

Mitchell smiled and backed away, holding his hands up in surrender. "Okay, okay, I get it. You're awfully touchy about her. Funny, you weren't that pissed when you found out about Bettina."

Mitchell sauntered off and Evan turned away, angry that he'd let his brother goad him.

"Evan, there you are."

He sighed when his mom latched on to his arm and dragged him over to introduce him to people he had zero interest in and would never see again in his life. After several minutes of pleasantries, Evan grew restless. The song ended, and he turned in search of Celia.

His father was making his way through the crowd toward Evan and Lucy, but Celia was nowhere to be seen. Frowning, Evan scanned the room until finally he found her.

She was dancing with Mitchell. She didn't look altogether thrilled, but Mitchell was smiling as he held Celia close.

Irrational anger exploded over Evan. All he could see was that it was Bettina all over again, only this time it mattered. This was Celia. His Celia.

His brother was a slimy predator. Never mind that Celia was perfectly capable of fending off any advances. He didn't even imagine she'd ever be receptive to an overture on Mitchell's part. But the fact that his brother would behave this way at his own wedding celebration enraged Evan.

His woman. He let Bettina go because she was never his. Celia was his even if she hadn't recognized that little fact.

Not stopping to think how it would look to others, he cut a path through the crowd that had people exclaiming on either side of him. When he got to Mitchell and Celia, he reached for his brother's arm and spun him around.

"What the—" Mitchell began.

His eyes narrowed angrily, but Evan stopped him with a look.

"You'll excuse us, Mitchell. I find I've spent entirely too much time away from my fiancée."

Celia stared at both brothers in shock but didn't utter a single protest when Evan all but dragged her out of the ballroom and into the hallway.

The predator had been unleashed. No way he'd stand by and watch his brother move in on what he considered his.

He stalked toward the elevator, his only thought to get Celia as far away from everyone else as possible. He punched the button and hauled her inside. As soon as the door closed, he slammed her against the back wall and angled his mouth over hers.

It was like a fuse igniting. Desire sizzled down his spine, frying every nerve ending in its path. He wasn't gentle. He wasn't sure he had it in him. He devoured her. Claimed her.

She gasped for breath, and he stole it as soon as she could gain it back.

"Evan, what on earth…"

The question ended on a moan as his mouth slid down her jaw to her neck. He sucked hungrily at the soft skin just below her ear.

Behind him the doors opened and without taking his mouth from her skin, he maneuvered them down the hall toward their suite.

He was on fire. He had no rational thought. His only instinct was to take her. To make her understand she belonged to him. Only to him.

Her eyes were dazed when he leaned her against the wall next to the door. His hands shook as he rummaged in his pocket for the key. It took two times before he inserted it correctly and as soon as the lock released, he threw open the door, held it with his foot and reached for her again.

This time she did her share of grabbing. Amid the turmoil of his jumbled, raging lust, relief hit him hard. She was with him. She wanted him every bit as much as he wanted her.

He tore at her clothing. Then he tore at his. Shoes and shirts hit the floor, leaving a trail across the floor to his bedroom.

By the time the backs of her knees hit the edge of his bed, she was down to just her bra and panties. Not just underwear. Pink, delicate, frothy confections that accentuated every curve and swell. Her breasts bulged and plumped upward over the cups. He could see a hint of her areola and it was driving him crazy.

His fingers fumbled with his pants. Her hands tangled with his as they both shoved downward.

"God, Celia." He couldn't catch his breath long enough to say what he wanted. "I always swore when I made love to you I'd savor you for hours. I told myself I'd take my time touching and kissing every inch of your body. But I swear, if I don't get inside you soon, I'm going to explode."

"Fast is good," she panted. "We can do slow later."

"Thank God."

He fell forward, taking her with him. They both hit the bed, and she absorbed the shock of his body melding to hers.

"I'll savor you next time," he promised between kisses.

"Savor is good. We can definitely savor. But, God, Evan, make love to me now. Please."

He chuckled and captured her mouth with his. "Sweet. So sweet. I'm going to take you, Celia. I'm going to take everything you have to offer. If you don't want this, tell me now. I'll stop. It'll kill me, but I'll stop."

She pulled away and stared up at him with glowing, brilliant eyes. Her hands traced a line from his temples over his face and to his jaw.

"Take me then," she whispered.

Ten

Celia lay underneath Evan's big body. Every part of her was covered by him. His heat penetrated her, seeped into her flesh and whispered seductively through her veins.

She wanted him. God, she wanted this man. Her need for him frightened and exhilarated her in equal parts. She knew she shouldn't—that she mustn't—and yet she also knew she wouldn't tell him no.

There would be no recriminations later. There would be no regret. She knew the potential pitfalls of making love with Evan, and she would face them with full acceptance.

"What are you thinking?" he asked.

She raised her gaze to meet his. He was propped on his arms, his body still flush with hers and their noses were mere inches apart.

His eyes were warm with desire, liquid with want, and her heart fluttered in response.

His voice was so tender and understanding. He stared down at her like she was the only woman he'd ever made love to. A mixture of awe and wonder that humbled her.

"I was thinking we shouldn't do this," she admitted.

"But? There's definitely a but in that sentence."

He sounded so hopeful that she smiled and once again traced the lean lines of his face with a fingertip.

"But I don't care. I should care. I should be on my way back to San Francisco. I should have never agreed to stay."

"But," he murmured again, his voice husky and so very predatory.

"But I'm here, in your arms, and I want you so much that I'm willing to take the biggest risk of my life. I won't lie, I don't like that about myself. I don't like that I'm allowing infatuation and sexual desire to mess with my head. It's stupid and irresponsible and…"

He shushed her with one finger and then followed it down with his lips. He nibbled playfully at the corner of her mouth and then licked the spot where he nipped.

"Trust me, Celia."

She went completely still and stared up at him, the intensity that burned so bright in his gaze.

"Trust me to take care of you. I won't let this hurt you. We can make it work."

"What are you saying?" she whispered.

"Let's take it slow. Well, after we go really fast this time." He grinned crookedly and shifted so she could feel his straining erection against her groin. "We can do this, Celia. We're adults in charge of our own destiny. There's no problem we can't solve together. Trust me."

Peace descended, enveloping her in its sweet, soothing grasp. In response, she wrapped her arms around his neck and tugged him down into a long, passionate kiss.

Trust him.

He made it sound so simple, and maybe it was.

She slid her mouth up his jaw to his ear. As she nibbled on it, she said softly, "Make love to me, Evan."

With a groan, he rolled until their positions were reversed and she was sprawled atop him. His fingers fumbled with the clasp of her bra and a second later, it flew across the room, hitting the drawn curtains over the window.

She felt his sudden inhalation. He stilled and then his hand skimmed up her back and around to her breasts. His fingertips brushed over the swells and to her nipples.

Each stroke, each touch no matter how light, ignited a

fire deep inside that threatened to overtake her. Her urgency matched his own. Her impatience was his.

And then he leaned up and took one sensitive nipple in his mouth and she was lost. Her head fell back. Her eyes closed as sweet, sharp pleasure radiated in waves through her body.

Despite his impatience, his lips and tongue were exquisitely tender as he suckled first one breast and then the other.

His hands spanned her waist and then moved lower until his fingers caught in the band of her panties. He yanked, and she heard them rip.

"I'll buy you more," he rasped as he rolled again, putting her underneath him once more.

"Buy me what?"

"Panties."

"Highly overrated," she murmured.

He laughed against her mouth. "I totally agree."

"Speaking of…underwear. You're still wearing yours."

He reared up between her knees, yanked his briefs off, and she stared shamelessly at his distended length. He followed her gaze down then looked back up at her, a cocky grin making him adorable.

"You like?"

She reached for him, enfolding him in her hands. "Oh, yes, I like."

He clamped a hand over her arm and squeezed. "Celia, you can't. I'm too close. This will never work. I have to get inside you or it's going to be over way too soon."

She rose up, curling one hand around his neck even as she slid her fingers suggestively up and down his erection.

"Savor later. Remember?"

"Condom," he bit out.

She let him go long enough for him to fumble through

his discarded pants. Seconds later, he started to roll the latex on, but she reached for it, snagging it from his grasp.

"Come here."

"Oh, yes, ma'am," he breathed.

She lay back and he straddled her hips. He loomed over her, big and strong. She felt entirely too small, too at his mercy, but as her hands slid over his manhood, he closed his eyes and a shudder rippled through his massive body, and the power shifted significantly in her direction.

Then he fell forward, planting his hands on either side of her head. "I can't wait."

"Savor later," she reminded.

His smile was brilliant. He leaned down to kiss her just as he reached down to part her thighs. With one hand, he pulled one leg away from the other. His mouth never left hers. His weight was supported by his left arm. He angled to the side as he gently explored her swollen, feminine folds.

"Evan, please," she begged. "You're killing me here. If you don't hurry, I'm so leaving you behind."

He eased one finger inside and evidently satisfied that she was ready for him, he shifted over her and settled between her thighs. His erection prodded carefully at first, then he found her heat and thrust hard and deep.

She arched, bowing her back off the mattress. She grasped desperately at his shoulders, her fingers curling into his skin until she was sure she drew blood.

It was too much. It was absolutely magnificent. He filled her. She'd never felt so alive, so splendid, so tuned in to her own pleasure.

"Hold on to me," he ordered in a thick, hazy voice.

It was a needless command. She couldn't do anything but hold him as he drove into her over and over.

"Oh," she gasped. "Evan, please, I need…"

She didn't even know what she was asking for, only that

she'd die if she didn't get it. Her body was near to breaking point. All she needed was…

He reached down and his fingers slid between them.

"That. Oh my God, that."

Her cry echoed sharply over the room. It was the single
most exquisite pleasure and pain all in one she'd experienced in her life. The tension was so sharp, so unbearable
and then finally she exploded.

The room darkened around her. She blinked but everything was fuzzy. All she was aware of was Evan stroking
into her and the wonderful melting sensation as she went
liquid around him.

He growled her name and then he gathered her in his
arms, holding her so tight she couldn't breathe. His hips
jerked against her before finally he collapsed onto her, his
chest heaving with exertion.

Her hands relaxed on his shoulders and went from pun-
ishing grip to soothing caresses. His skin was damp, and
all that could be heard were his harsh breaths against her
neck.

She held him as tight as he held her, determined to
offer him all of herself. No barriers. No defenses. Just two
people connecting in a way that overwhelmed her senses.

"You undo me, Celia," he said, his voice muffled against
her neck.

She smiled and continued to stroke his back, enjoying
the feel of his flesh beneath her fingers.

He finally rolled away to discard the condom and then
came back and pulled her into his arms so they faced
each other.

"That was…amazing."

She touched his lips, still fascinated with the feel of
him, the rougher textures and the softness of his mouth.

"I felt pretty savored."

He smiled and kissed her, just one light smooch that sent a giddy little thrill down her back.

"I have this fantasy. It's pretty vivid, actually."

"This I gotta hear."

He smacked her lightly on her behind. "Listen up, woman. Pay attention when your man bears his soul."

She laughed and he continued.

"It didn't quite go according to plan because I was supposed to savor you first. I planned to take a couple of hours and make love to you until you were mindless. Then I was going to take you hard and fast."

"Screwed that one up."

He smacked her again and shook his head.

"So now I have this fantasy where we have fast and furious sex. Then I savor you for…okay maybe an hour. And then we have fast, furious sex again. Then you get on top and have your wicked way with me. And then you get on your hands and knees…"

Celia put her hand over his mouth and burst out laughing. "Okay, okay, I get the picture. You're an insatiable, horny male."

"Only for you," he said seriously. "You seem to regularly star in my most-vivid fantasies. I could probably be arrested for some of them. They might not be legal in all states."

"Lucky for you, California is so progressive," she murmured.

Her heart fluttered helplessly. His words… God, his words. How could she even respond to what he'd said? He sounded so…sincere. How had they gotten to this point? It scared the living hell out of her.

"So what about you? Have any interesting fantasies about me?"

He sounded so hopeful that she had to laugh again. She

leaned forward and brushed her mouth against the muscled wall of his chest.

"I'm liking the savor part a lot."

"Me, too," he murmured as he reached down to tug her chin high enough that he could kiss her again.

He was a man of his word. He spent every bit of the next hour driving her mindless with his hands and his mouth. His tongue. Have mercy, his tongue.

There wasn't an inch of her he left untouched. He put his stamp on her. She felt branded. Possessed.

His tongue circled her most sensitive point nestled among the soft folds of her femininity. He worked her to the very brink of orgasm, until she quivered uncontrollably. She shivered when he pulled away and then finally he slid into her, long and slow. Hot and so tender. So very tender.

She squeezed her eyes shut but then he pressed gentle kisses to her lids until she opened them again. He stared down at her with such intensity she forgot to breathe. His eyes burned a fiery trail over her face, stroking and caressing her cheeks and her mouth.

He was dangerous. Oh, yes, so dangerous. She had no protection from him, and worse, she didn't want any. He could easily find his way into her heart.

Maybe he already had.

That should scare her to death, but instead, a warm, comfortable feeling settled over her. Contentment.

She stared into his eyes and saw herself. Saw them. Together.

He rocked over her, taking his time as he stoked the fire inside her higher and higher.

The strain was evident on his face. He held himself in check as he drove her relentlessly toward release. He wasn't going to let go of his own until she reached hers.

She twined her body tightly with his, loving the sensation of being so connected, so intrinsically linked.

"Evan," she whispered against his mouth.

He kissed her. Hard. "Give it to me. Let go."

The breathless words unlocked something deep inside her. She arched into him, giving herself unreservedly. Wave after wave of the most beautiful pleasure rolled through her, fanning out and rippling.

He groaned and followed until she wasn't sure whose pleasure was whose and where hers began and ended.

He eased down, and she welcomed him into her arms. She pillowed his head on her chest, his mouth a breath away from her nipple. He kissed the plump swell of her breast but didn't move. Their hearts thudded against each other and neither did anything to break the silence.

What could be said? She knew she didn't have words. She didn't want to dissect the moment. Words would only ruin the euphoric aftermath of an experience she was at a loss to describe anyway.

She ran her hand idly through his mussed hair. At his nape the crisp hairs were slightly damp with sweat. She inhaled, savoring the uniquely masculine smell of sex and sweat. It was intoxicating and erotic.

"Does it make me a bastard that I'm already fantasizing about the part where you climb on top of me and have your wicked way?" he mumbled against her chest.

She smiled. "As soon as I regain the feeling in my legs, I'll see what I can do about that particular fantasy."

Eleven

Waking in bed with Evan didn't bring about the immediate what-the-hell-have-I-done feeling she would have thought. No, when her eyes opened, she registered a fantastic male body wrapped around hers, and instead of shoving him over and wailing on about how dumb she was, she snuggled deeper into his embrace and soaked up every minute of the lazy morning.

"Good morning," Evan murmured against her temple.

"Mmm."

He chuckled softly and rolled away for a moment.

"Damn."

"I don't like that damn," she grumbled. "Bad things are going to happen after that word."

He sighed in regret. "Sorry. Yeah, we have to get up."

"What time is it?"

"Noon."

Her eyes popped open and she scrambled up to look over his body at the clock.

"Noon? I've never slept until noon in my life!"

He grinned and tugged her down onto his chest. "Glad I could contribute to your downfall then."

"So arrogant," she said. "Now let me go, otherwise I'll look like a bag lady for your brother's wedding."

"I like bag ladies."

She snorted. "Ladies carrying Hermes Berkin bags maybe."

He gave her a puzzled look that suggested he didn't have

a clue what she was talking about. She rolled her eyes and then pried herself out of his arms.

"Come on, get up," she coaxed. "The sooner we get it over with, the sooner you can see your brother and his new wife on their way, and we can go home."

He threw off the covers, and she nearly squeaked as he got up from the bed, stark naked. Then she realized that she wasn't any more clothed, and she fled for the bathroom, his laughter ringing in her ears.

Two hours later, dressed appropriately, they made their way to the terrace where the lovebirds would exchange their vows. As they reached the door leading out, Evan slipped an arm around her waist and pulled her close to his side.

Warmth spread through her cheeks until she remembered that this was all for show. She'd been stupid to forget that even for a moment.

When navigating the chairs and the people mingling became too difficult, he loosened his hold on her waist and tucked her hand in his instead. His fingers laced with hers and his thumb rubbed her palm as he smiled and said his hellos.

The preceremony was a bit of a madhouse and was without structure. Everyone just gathered on the terrace overlooking the cozy inlet, talking and visiting until finally Evan's father stood close to the floral arch and raised his hands for attention.

"If everyone will take their seats, I believe we're ready to begin."

Evan led Celia to the front row where they sat beside Lucy and Marshall. Evan kept a firm hold on her hand until Bettina made her appearance.

Despite his seeming indifference, Evan's demeanor changed as soon as the ceremony began. His fingers loosened from hers until she drew her hand away to rest in her own lap. He made no move to prevent the action.

His gaze was locked on Bettina and his brother, and he wasn't smiling as the rest of the attendees were. He looked like a stone pillar. No emotion.

What made it worse was when Lucy started sending sidelong glances at Evan. She'd obviously picked up on his coldness.

It begged the question as to whether Evan was as unaffected as he'd reported. Did he still love Bettina? If he was to be believed, he never had, but then did a man like Evan fall in love?

His association with Bettina could hardly be deemed romantic. He'd formed a shopping list for a prospective bride and he hadn't looked far. The first suitable candidate he'd found he put a ring on her finger and that was that.

Celia glanced down at the diamond gleaming on her third finger and winced.

Oh, Celia, tell me you haven't gotten caught up in this nonsense. You're too practical.

She almost snorted. When it came to Evan, practicality didn't crop up first. Or second or even third. She'd lusted after forbidden fruit from the moment she'd seen him.

A tiny, unwelcome thought niggled at her consciousness. Would she have begged so hard to be the one to pitch to Evan if she hadn't been so fascinated with him? Another derisive sound had to be stifled. Fascination was a very tame word to describe her fixation with Evan. Attracted. That wasn't a very descriptive word, either. It seemed no matter the word, it didn't do justice to the overwhelming barrage of sensations she experienced in his presence.

Thank God the weekend was almost over and she could hopefully gain some objectivity again. This ruse of theirs was a dangerous fantasy for her. If she didn't remove herself from it immediately, she was going to fall complete victim to it.

She could just see trying to explain that to her boss. The boss who had put his company's fate in her hands.

And then the ceremony was over and suddenly Evan was smiling down at her once more. She promptly forgot all about her worries and reservations.

Once again he was attentive. He touched her frequently as if he couldn't keep his hands off her. It made her nuts the way her body leaped to life under his attention, but she couldn't control it.

As they waited behind the line of people going back inside, Evan leaned down and nuzzled her ear.

"Let's go have some fun at the reception," he murmured. "You, me, a little dirty dancing..."

She laughed as the tightness left her chest. It was hard to remember all the reasons she shouldn't become involved with this man when he charmed her to her toes.

She tucked her hand willingly in his, and this time she curled her fingers around his as he led her into the hotel. No, logically she shouldn't immerse herself in this charade. But then attraction was anything but logical. She had only a few more hours before she would be jolted back to reality. She planned to enjoy every single one of them.

They danced. Slow, sensual songs and even the more upbeat tunes. Evan was astonishingly adept as he spun her around the room. Somehow she hadn't seen him as the type to do more than a staid waltz or just a slow cuddle type dance in the middle of the floor.

She should have known. The man was a study in athletic grace.

They took a quick break and Evan left Celia to go get drinks for them both. Celia turned to see Lucy approaching through the crowd, her face lit up like a Christmas tree.

"Celia! I'm so glad I got over to you before Evan spirits you away again."

Celia smiled warmly back at Evan's mother.

Lucy reached out to squeeze Celia's hand. "I can't thank you enough for coming. It's so obvious that the two of you are in love."

It took everything Celia had not to react to that statement. Obvious? How could it be? In lust, yes, but love? Evan would be horrified that his farce had worked a little too well. Nothing like a rumor of being in love to scare off the opposite sex. A man like Evan probably had more women than he could shake a stick at.

But he didn't take any of them to the wedding. He'd taken her.

Business, Celia reminded herself. It was convenient and business had been at the forefront of his mind.

"The two of you make such a lovely couple," Lucy said wistfully. "I do hope you'll agree to a wedding date soon. Don't make him wait, even though I'm sure he deserves it. I want him to be happy."

"I'm sure the both of us will come up with a mutually satisfactory date," Celia said diplomatically.

Lucy squeezed again and then suddenly Celia found herself enveloped in the older woman's arms.

"It was a joy to have you here, Celia. I can't wait to see you again."

Lucy drew away, beaming at Celia the entire time, and Celia felt like the lowest form of pond scum for her part in deceiving this woman.

"Oh, look, there's Evan with your drink. I'll disappear now and let you two get back to your fun."

Lucy blew a kiss in Evan's direction and melted back into the crowd.

"What was that all about?" Evan asked as he approached.

He handed her a wineglass and stepped in close, their bodies touching.

Celia grimaced. "She was telling me how wonderful she thought it was that we're getting married."

"Ah, well, that would explain the look of torture in your eyes."

He slid his arm around her waist and pulled her close. He stared down into her eyes, and then he simply kissed her.

Stunned that he would be so public, even when perpetuating a hoax, she stood there in the circle of his arms while he kissed her senseless.

Desire unfurled and spread rapid fire through her belly. All he had to do was kiss her and she was helpless to do anything more than respond.

"You know, we have late check-out," he murmured against her lips. "Very late check-out. My jet can leave at my ready. What do you say we go back to the room?"

No. They needed to return home. She needed the weekend to be over so she could recover her sanity. But instead of no, she opened her mouth and whispered, "yes."

The predatory gleam was back in his eyes. He put both their glasses down on a nearby table and then he took her hand and all but dragged her from the reception. They ran down the hallway to the elevator like two hormonally imbalanced teenagers.

When they reached the room, he threw open the door, swung her into his arms and carried her straight to the bedroom. He plopped her down on the bed and stood back as he tore out of his clothes.

She leaned up on one elbow to stare appreciatively at his physique.

"You know," she said coyly. "There is one of your fantasies we haven't played out yet."

His eyebrows shot up and then he crawled onto the bed until he loomed menacingly over her.

"Oh, really. Which one?"

She circled her arms around his neck and pulled him down into a kiss. Then she slid her mouth to his ear to whisper in shocking detail exactly which fantasy she was talking about.

Evan's plane landed in San Francisco close to midnight. He helped her down the steps onto the tarmac and stood next to her as they waited for his car to pull forward.

He touched her cheek, pushing aside a stray strand of hair. In truth, she looked and felt disheveled from head to toe. What had started as a quick interlude had turned into an afternoon of wanton, hedonistic pleasure. They'd made love more times than she could count.

They'd stumbled out of the hotel looking like a pair of illicit lovers hurrying back to their spouses after a hot weekend affair.

She shook her head to clear that notion. There was nothing dishonorable about her liaison with Evan. It was separate from business, she asserted firmly. Separate.

"Are you sure you won't let me escort you home?" Evan asked.

He glanced between her and the car that was now parked a few feet away, and his lips were drawn into a fine line.

She shook her head. "No, you still have to fly back to Seattle, and it's already past midnight. I'll be fine. Your driver will take good care of me."

He looked as if he was going to press the point when she raised her hand. The diamond caught the glare from the headlights. Slowly she removed the thin band from her finger and pressed the ring into Evan's palm.

"I won't be needing this anymore," she said lightly.

He frowned as he stared down at the delicate piece of jewelry lying in his hand.

It was ridiculous that this felt like a real break-up. Her heart seized and she had the absurd urge to snatch the ring back out of his hand and put it back on her finger.

She leaned up on tiptoe and brushed her lips across his cheek. "Goodbye, Evan. Have a safe trip home."

She turned and allowed the driver to usher her into the backseat. As they pulled away, she saw Evan standing in the same place she'd left him, his hand closed around the ring. They stared at each other through the window until the car got too far away for her to see him any longer.

Twelve

Evan tucked his hand into his pocket to touch the diamond engagement ring Celia had given back to him the night before. His finger ran over the edges, took it out and let it lay in his palm to catch the light.

For a long while, he stared down at it before closing his hand over it. As his driver pulled to the curb in front of Maddox Communications, he shoved the ring back into his pocket.

Celia wouldn't be expecting him. Hell, he wasn't expecting him. To be here, that is. He was supposed to have flown back to Seattle. He had any number of issues to deal with including talking to his team about Noah Hart. They needed to come big with an offer, and they needed to make sure any offer they made was tied up neatly with a big bow.

Yet, here he was, getting out at Celia's building because he wanted to see her again. And business had nothing to do with it.

He instructed his driver to find suitable parking and to swing back around when he phoned to say he was ready. Then he headed into the stately building to take the elevator up to the sixth floor.

When he stepped off, he was immediately impressed with the very modern, "in touch" feel of Maddox Communications. There was a lot of attention given to comfort, and it worked, because he felt relaxed.

Two large-screen plasma televisions were positioned on either side of the large reception desk, and Maddox's latest ad campaigns were predominately displayed in a series of commercials.

Behind the desk, a cheerful looking younger woman smiled a warm welcome as he approached.

"Good morning and welcome to Maddox Communications."

He returned her smile. "Can you tell Celia Taylor that Evan Reese is here to see her?"

The sudden awareness in the receptionist's eyes told him she knew well who he was. She recovered quickly, though. With brisk efficiency, she rounded the corner of her desk and gestured toward the set of couches in the waiting area.

"If you'll have a seat, I'll get her at once. Would you care for some coffee?"

"No, thank you."

She turned to stride down the hallway, leaving Evan standing there. He walked to the window to look down on the street instead of sitting. If he had his way, he wouldn't be here for long anyway.

A few moments later, he heard the tap tap of heels and turned to see Celia approaching, a confused, wary look in her eyes.

"Evan," she greeted. "I wasn't expecting to see you. I thought you were going back to Seattle. Is anything wrong?"

She'd put her impersonal business face on the moment he looked up. It annoyed him that she was pushing him away, already distancing herself from the weekend they'd shared. It should be him doing the pushing. He should have gotten her out of his system after making love to her more times than he could count.

But he hadn't, which was why he found himself standing here, trying to come up with an excuse to see her again.

"Nothing's wrong. My plans changed. I thought we could have lunch. If you're free, that is."

She checked her watch, a quick, nervous motion that told him she was merely stalling—and trying to think of an excuse why she couldn't.

"I would very much like to have lunch with you, Celia."

Her forehead wrinkled in indecision. She nibbled at her bottom lip. He took advantage of that moment to move closer until he crowded her. Before she could take a step back, he grasped her arm.

Alarm flared in her eyes, and she broke the contact, stepping hastily away as she stared wildly in all directions.

"For God's sake, Evan, not here," she hissed.

Her hand trembled as she raised one to smooth her hair. Instead of repairing the knot, she only managed to work more strands free. They fell down her neck, calling attention to the slim column. He was reminded of all the time he'd spent nibbling at that sweet flesh.

He raised an eyebrow at her vehemence but kept his distance.

"Lunch?"

"All right. Let me get my purse. I'll meet you downstairs."

Her dismissal rankled him. He was used to calling the shots when it came to women and relationships.

Hell, now he was thinking of her in terms of a relationship? The only thing he should be thinking was how quickly he could get her back into bed so that hopefully this time he'd get rid of the burning ache he felt when she crossed his mind.

Crossed. What a funny word, one that denoted an occasional, unintentional meeting. She lived in his mind. He didn't like it, didn't particularly care for the implication, but he was powerless to rid himself of her assault on his senses.

He stared at her for a long moment, and only because he was convinced she was ready to bolt, did he acquiesce.

"All right. I'll call my driver around. Oh, and Celia. I don't like to be kept waiting."

Celia spun around before she exploded. She wished she could blame it all on her anger and his arrogance, but she'd been flabbergasted when Shelby had rushed into her office to tell her Evan Reese was here and he wanted to see her.

The giddy thrill that sizzled down her spine annoyed her. And then his arrogant presumption that she'd drop everything to have lunch with him. He didn't like to be kept waiting. Who did he think he was?

She sighed as she collected her purse. Where to even begin? He was an important client. The most important client of her career. And then there was the fact she'd acted as his fake fiancée, and oh yeah, she'd slept with him. Repeatedly.

A hot blush shot up her neck and nearly burned her cheeks off as she remembered just how often they'd had sex. They'd re-enacted all his fantasies and some of hers, too.

They'd been insatiable.

Hell and damnation but she'd expected several days to recover from the weekend before she had to see him again. In her utter befuddlement and not to mention being blown over by the sex, she hadn't even mentioned the season opener to Evan.

It was as good an excuse as any to accompany him to lunch. At least then she could pretend it was all about business.

After a quick wave to Shelby, she rode the elevator down to the first floor. She passed the busy American cuisine restaurant with the lunch crowd lined up at the door and exited the building.

Evan was standing at the curb, one hand resting on the

open door to the backseat of his car, the other shoved into his pocket. He looked positively arrogant. Like he not only belonged in the world but owned it.

He nodded as she approached and motioned her inside the car. Then he slid in beside her and shut the door.

"I thought we could eat at this restaurant I know across town. It's small and not so well-known, but the food is excellent and it affords privacy."

He looked at her almost like the last was a challenge.

She tilted her chin up and stared coolly at him. She hoped that she looked as unruffled as she wanted to portray.

"Is this business, Evan? Why did you come to my office today?"

His mouth tightened briefly before he relaxed and eyed her with thinly veiled amusement.

"We slept together, Celia. I don't think lunch is that scandalous given that fact."

She curled her fingers into tight fists. She wanted to close her eyes and moan her dismay. No, she doubted he'd understand why it was so important to her that there be no hint of impropriety between them. He was the type who'd never let what others thought rule his life. She hated that evidently she was the type. Hated it but couldn't change it.

"Evan."

She stopped when her voice cracked. She felt like the worst sort of idiot. Around others she had no problem being blunt—and forceful when the occasion called for it. But with Evan, she was ridiculously tongue-tied.

"Yes?" he prompted.

He wore a curious smile, almost as if he found her and the situation amusing. It made her angry.

"We can't do this. We simply can't. This weekend was a huge mistake. I don't want to be one of these women who say no, no, no, and then yes, yes, yes and then spend the next week castigating myself for my weakness. I shouldn't have slept with you. I swear, I left my brain behind when we went to Catalina. I knew what I was getting into. Don't get me wrong. I don't blame you or think you manipulated me into having sex with you. I'm a big girl and I knew full well what I was doing. It doesn't make me any less stupid, mind you."

Evan simply hauled her into his arms and stifled her tirade with a kiss. Not just any kiss. He devoured her whole. She melted—positively melted—in his arms. She went limp against him.

Yep, she was one of those silly women at the mercy of her hormones.

She placed both hands on his chest and shoved until they sat apart, both breathing raggedly. She probably looked demented sitting there, hair askew, chest heaving up and down as if she'd run a marathon.

"Stop kissing me!"

He smiled again, a lazy, sensual smile of a lion standing over its prey. She was lunch apparently.

"But I like kissing you and I try never to deny myself life's little pleasures."

She rolled her eyes then caught herself before she laughed.

"Dammit, Evan. Be serious for one minute. I mean it. Stop kissing me and stop touching me."

He held his hands up in surrender. "Okay, okay. I won't touch you."

She crossed her arms protectively over her chest and moved as far over in the seat as she could. Why had she agreed to lunch with him? Why?

Because you're a masochist and you can't resist him.

There was that.

She'd always thought it was a myth. The out-of-control hormones that made an otherwise intelligent woman make waste of her brain cells every time she came into contact with the one.

She was certainly proving the waste of brain cells to be true.

The rest of the journey was spent in brooding silence. Evan was silent and Celia brooded. When they finally pulled up to a restaurant that boasted the best seafood on the west coast, she raised a skeptical eyebrow.

"Try it first and then tell me if you disagree," Evan said in amusement.

He was becoming way too adept at reading her and it annoyed her to no end, especially since she had no idea what went on in his head. She was afraid to find out.

When she stepped out and glanced around, she had to hand it to him. For a man who didn't seemingly care if they were seen together or not and certainly didn't have the objections she had, he'd chosen a restaurant where they weren't likely to be seen by anyone who knew them.

Evan guided her in to the rustic cedar building with its quasi-southern charm mixed with California décor. It was an odd blend that, to her surprise, worked well.

The two sat in the far corner where the lighting so was so dim a small kerosene lantern sat in the middle of the table to offer ambience.

"I feel like I'm on a first date," she said ruefully after Evan had ordered the wine.

He smiled and waggled his eyebrows suggestively. "Would it make me less of a jerk to be up front about the fact I plan to have you in my bed tonight?"

She sucked in her breath until she felt curiously light-headed. She suspected of course, but to hear him say it outright was way sexier than it should have been.

"I have to go back to work," she murmured.

He nodded. "Of course. I didn't intend to spirit you

away for an afternoon tryst, though the idea has merit. I wonder if your coworkers would call the police?"

She glared at him—determined not to laugh. But even her scowl twitched. Irreverent bastard.

The waiter appeared with food, and she blinked because she hadn't remembered ordering. She glanced at the half-empty wineglass and couldn't for the life of her remember drinking so much as a sip. Evan was bad, bad for her brain. He was as bad as some wasting disease. She wouldn't survive, either.

"Evan," she began again, and promptly shut up when it came out more as a plaintive wail than a protest.

"I'll send a car for you, Celia. No one needs to see you getting into a vehicle with me. I'll have my driver pick you up from work, or if you prefer, you can drive your car to your apartment and I'll have him pick you up there. And I'll have him take you home in time for you to prepare for work."

Why wasn't she immediately shutting him down? Instead of telling him that in no uncertain terms would she agree to such a thing, she found herself contemplating how decadent it would be to dash off to an elicit rendezvous with her lover.

She shivered at the word *lover*. Evan was a superb specimen of a man. He was fantastic in bed and insatiable to boot. He knew how to pleasure a woman and was as unselfish a lover as she'd ever had. The mere idea of spending the night with him had her tied in so many knots it would take a team of massage therapists to work them out.

She chewed absently at the food, not registering the taste or even what she ate. Her throat was as dry as the desert and her tongue was swollen and clumsy.

"You act as though it's a crime for us to make love," he said in an oddly tender voice.

If it had been coaxing or wheedling, she could have

been cold to him. But she could swear he was reassuring her and attempting to allay her fears.

She licked her lips and raised her gaze to meet his. Awareness hit her square in the chest. In his eyes she saw undulating bodies. Hers and his. In perfect rhythm. So beautiful and so pleasurable that she closed her eyes to further immerse herself in the memory.

"Say yes."

His voice stroked her as surely as his fingers had done. A prickle of goose bumps spread rapidly over her shoulders and down her chest until her nipples tightened into two painful knots.

"Celia," he prompted.

Finally she opened her eyes and fixed him with her unfocused gaze.

"Yes," she whispered.

Thirteen

Celia entered her office with a heightened sense of anticipation. She already knew she'd be clock watching until it was quitting time and then she'd race home so she could change and look her best for her naughty escape to Evan's.

Her mouth curved into a naughty smile to match the naughtiness of her and Evan's plan. It was wicked, forbidden, and she was so turned on that she was ready to fidget right out of her shoes.

With a sigh, she sank into her chair behind her desk, kicked off her shoes and logged on to catch up on e-mail. She hadn't planned to go out for lunch at all and had, in fact, brought food from home, planning to eat at her desk. After missing Friday, she'd spent the morning getting a report from Jason on her client meetings he covered and then she'd gone through messages.

She groaned as her in-box stacked up with e-mail after e-mail. She started at the bottom and worked up, deleting several after cursory glances. Those requiring a lengthy response she flagged to respond to later and the ones she could just do a one-line response to she typed furiously and sent on their way.

She was nearly to the end when her gaze flickered over the name Lucy Reese. She did a double take. Evan's mom? Why would she e-mail and how had she gotten Celia's address?

Her stomach fluttered a bit, and guilt crept over her all over again. Lucy was nice and Celia hated lying to her.

She hated lying as a rule for any reason but especially not for such a frivolous endeavor.

She braced herself and clicked on the message. It began as cheerfully as Lucy herself was in person. She said again how thrilled she was that Celia and Evan had found each other.

Talk about another shot to the gut.

She expressed her desire to see Celia again and hoped Evan would bring her to Seattle for a visit.

Could this get any worse?

Her message ended with a short note that she'd attached some pictures from the wedding that she thought Celia would enjoy.

Celia opened the attached JPEGs and couldn't help but smile. The pictures were of her and Evan at the wedding reception. They looked happy and…in love.

There was one of them dancing, another of Evan looking down with a tender expression and the last was when Evan had kissed her. Celia's hand rested on his chest and the glitter of the ring contrasted with the black of Evan's tuxedo. Their mouths were fused together, and it was obvious to anyone looking at the picture that they were in danger of combusting right there in the middle of a crowded reception.

For several minutes, she debated whether or not to reply to Lucy's e-mail. It seemed rude not to, but it was also a terrible thing to prolong the charade.

Finally, she settled for a brief thank you and that she'd enjoyed meeting Lucy, as well. It was true and didn't delve into any part of her nonexistent relationship with Evan.

Stealing over to the man's hotel room after work hours certainly couldn't be considered a relationship.

Her intercom beeped, startling her from her thoughts.

"Celia, I have a cleaning service willing to take over Noah Hart's house."

"Brave," Celia muttered.

"What was that?"

"Nothing. Do you have details on when they'll start? Can you e-mail me that and the agency name and contact info so I can forward it?"

"Sure."

There was a distinct pause and then Shelby's hesitant voice filtered through the intercom.

"Sooo, are you going to give me the dirt on Noah Hart? Like how you know him and why you're arranging his maid service?"

"No," Celia said shortly.

She punched the button to end the conversation and hoped Shelby would get the hint. True, Shelby liked to gossip but she wasn't overtly intrusive. She backed off when people wanted her to.

She checked her e-mail and then forwarded the information to Noah. After closing her e-mail program, she stared at her phone and sighed. Noah was a disaster when it came to e-mails. The man just didn't care about advanced methods of communication. If it couldn't be said on the phone or in person, he wasn't much interested. It drove his agent nuts. Simon Blackstone much preferred the impersonal methods of e-mail and text messages to actual conversations, but if he wanted to talk to Noah, he had to pick up the phone. Celia was convinced Noah did it just to torque his agent's jaw.

At any rate, she'd better call and leave a message on Noah's cell or God knows what the cleaning lady would come across when she went to his house.

She'd hit the end button after leaving him a nagging, sisterly message when it hit her square in the face that she had neglected to mention the game to Evan.

How could she be so stupid? With everything else that had gone on in the weekend, the game had slipped her mind. Even when she'd done the pitch and specifically dangled the Noah carrot in front of Evan's nose, she'd flaked on the season opener.

He was probably already booked solid, if he was even going to be in town. The game was the night before her scheduled pitch session and he'd probably just fly in on the morning of their meeting.

"Stupid, stupid, stupid," she muttered.

Would it be crass to mention it tonight? During their little sex getaway? If she wanted to get him in front of Noah in a casual setting, then she was going to have to move fast and hope he hadn't locked up his week already with other obligations.

She looked up when a knock sounded at her door. Brock stood against the door frame, a smile easing the newly developed lines at his eyes and mouth.

"Hey, we wanted to get together at Rosa after work today. You're the star and we want to toast with copious amounts of alcohol. It will be a good pep rally for the presentation on Friday."

Her stomach rolled into a tight ball. The last thing she wanted was a raucous night at Rosa with the work gang. Usually she'd be all over it. The Maddox employees regularly hung out at the upscale martini bar just a block away. It's where they met to celebrate, commiserate or just take a break from a hellish workday.

The last celebration they'd staged there had been for Jason after he'd landed the Prentice account. Now Brock was lining up the chorus for her.

Her cheeks tightened in pleasure even as her heart sank at the idea of ditching Evan after agreeing to meet him. He'd think her the worst sort of coward even if it was the smart thing to do.

"I'd love to, Brock, but I already have plans for the evening. Important plans," she added after a pause. "Besides,

I'd rather not jinx myself before going into the presentation. It's not in the bag—yet—but I certainly plan to perform a slam dunk on Friday."

He nodded. "Yeah, I understand. We'll go and just call it a pre-planning session. It's as good an excuse as any to throw back a few. But if you land this, just be prepared for a victory celebration to end all victory celebrations."

She grinned. "Oh, you know it. I can't wait. I'll totally hold you to it."

"Okay, take care and see you tomorrow." He turned to go but stopped and turned back once more. "Oh, and, Celia, if I haven't already said it, thank you. You did a magnificent job. I doubted your approach at first, but you came through in spades."

Her heart sped up and she curled her fingers until her nails dug into her palms. It was all she could do not to stand up and throw her arms in the air complete with an obnoxious yell.

"Thank you for your trust," she said as calmly as possible.

With a short salute, he disappeared down the hallway, leaving Celia grinning like a loon.

Promptly at a quarter to five, Celia headed down the elevator—fifteen minutes before quitting time so she'd miss the majority of her coworkers. She didn't want to explain why she wasn't joining them at Rosa.

Her apartment wasn't far, and usually she'd enjoy driving her Beamer with the top down—it really was a sassy, smooth handling dream machine—but today she was just impatient to be home, and the traffic was driving her mad.

When she reached her apartment, she recognized the car out front and the driver standing on the curb beside it. With a groan, she slowed to a stop on the street and rolled down her window.

"I'll only be a moment," she called.

The driver smiled, tipped his hat and said, "No hurry, Miss Taylor. Take your time."

She maneuvered into her parking spot and dashed inside, ready to do battle. She hadn't missed Evan's reaction to her sexy, feminine lingerie. It was her one indulgence or what she deemed a silly indulgence since her sex life was so staid in the last few years that no one but her had a prayer of ever seeing what her underwear looked like.

Hopping on one foot as she stepped out of her clothing, she went over to her drawer to find the most sinful set of lingerie she owned. She settled on pink. What was more feminine or soft looking than pink? Even growing up with a horde of boys hadn't erased the girly from her. And since she was a redhead, wearing pink clothing wasn't an option. But pink underwear she could do.

Unsure of whether she'd return to her apartment before going to work the next day—and she did like to be prepared for anything—she threw an outfit into an overnight bag along with her toiletries and a lavender bra and panties.

She did a quick check of her messages and then did something she never did. She turned off her BlackBerry and tucked it into her overnight bag. Tonight was hers. She needed no reminders from the business world. If she was going to indulge in fantasy, she was going whole hog.

She locked up and hurried out her door to the street where the driver waited. He ushered her into the backseat and they drove away into traffic.

It amused her how exciting she found the whole experience. She could be a mistress at the beck and call of her über-wealthy benefactor, discreetly bundled into a private car and rushed to meet him at an undisclosed location.

"Get it together, Celia," she muttered.

Lord, but she did lose all her brain cells when it came to this man. If she wasn't careful, she'd throw away all her independence and start greeting him at the door every evening, wearing a kitchen apron with oven mitts and a piping-hot casserole dish.

Oddly, but the image wasn't all that distasteful. For the first few seconds anyway. She laughed outright and it had the effect of someone popping her thought bubble with a sharp pin.

The driver looked up in the rearview mirror, and she valiantly tried to look back with a straight face. If he only knew the absurd thoughts she was processing.

If she was truly the naughty girl of her fantasies, she would have ridden over with only a trench coat covering her sexy lingerie. Then when she walked into Evan's room, she could discard the coat and watch his reaction.

The idea certainly had merit, and if she ever received another invitation such as tonight, she'd give it serious consideration.

A few minutes later, the driver pulled up to the sumptuous hotel Evan resided in when he was in town, bypassed the main entrance and stopped at the second pull in where her door was immediately opened by one of the hotel staff.

Maybe Evan had his own entrance. The thought amused her, but then he had so much money, it wouldn't surprise her.

She was immediately met by the concierge and was handed a keycard.

"Mr. Reese wishes for you to go right up," the older man said.

She blushed from head to toe. She knew well what it looked like. Like she was some hooker or mistress—precisely what she'd imagined on her way over—all set to have a clandestine meeting.

She took the key card, murmured her thanks, and shot past the doorman and into the small hallway leading directly to the elevators. Thankfully she bypassed the lobby entirely. It seemed like everyone in the world knew what she was here for.

In the elevator, she inserted her key and punched the button for the top floor. She was whisked to the top in no time at all and stepped into the eerily quiet hallway. There were only a few doors. The rooms must be huge because she only counted four doors total. Evan's was on the very end, and she took a deep breath before inserting the key into the slot.

When she opened the door and stepped inside, she immediately saw Evan standing across the room, drink in hand, his eyes fixed on her. He'd been waiting. She could sense his impatience and see the triumph in his expression when she closed the door behind her.

She stood there, unmoving, as he put his drink aside and crossed the room in just a few, long strides.

"You came," he murmured.

He swept her into his arms and kissed her. He wasn't gentle or even particularly careful. Their bodies came together in a clash she felt all the way to her bones.

"Did you think I wouldn't?" she asked when she was finally able to draw a breath.

His eyes glittered, and his throat worked up and down as if he was trying to hold on to his control.

"If you hadn't, I was prepared to go and drag you out of your apartment."

All her concerns fell away. Nothing else mattered but the intense need they felt for each other.

"Next time I won't come. I have my own set of caveman fantasies wherein the Neanderthal drags me off to his cave."

He growled low in his throat and before she could react, he had her in his arms and was striding toward the bedroom.

Fourteen

They made it as far as the dresser. Evan slid her onto the polished surface of the wood and leaned in until she straddled his hips.

"I swore this time I'd savor first," he said against her mouth. "Dammit, but when I see you, all reason flies out the door."

She hooked her legs around his back and pulled him into the V of her groin.

"Has anyone ever told you that you talk too much?"

"Never a woman," he murmured as he swept hungrily over her mouth.

Her excitement mounted as Evan ripped at her shirt. He shoved it down over her shoulders, trapping her arms to her sides. His hands smoothed up her bare skin to her shoulders. He gripped her so hard, she knew she'd wear his prints.

His breath blew hot over her chin and then her jaw. He kissed a line to her ear then sucked the lobe between his teeth.

Shivers overtook her. Delicate little goose bumps dotted her flesh until she trembled uncontrollably.

He stepped back, his hands falling to the waistband of her pants. His fingers hung in the snap and he stood there staring at her heaving chest.

"You're so beautiful."

He raised one finger to hook in the strap of her bra. He

ran it up then down, and he grazed the tip over the swell of her breast.

"I love the lingerie."

She leaned back on the dresser, resting her palms on the top to give him a better glimpse of her cleavage.

"You're absolutely merciless, aren't you?" he murmured.

She smiled and arched invitingly until the barest hint of her nipples peeked at him over the lace cups of her bra.

He wrapped both arms around her waist and lowered his mouth to the valley between her breasts. He kissed and nibbled at the plump swells until she gasped and struggled for each breath.

The straps had loosened and tumbled down her shoulders. He slid his palms up her body, hooked his thumbs in the straps and dragged them back down.

He tugged until finally one cup slipped down and freed her breast. He licked the nipple until it puckered and strained outward. Then he closed his mouth ever so gently around the tip.

"Evan," she whispered as her hands tangled in his hair.

He sucked softly and then with more pressure until her entire focus was the streaks of pleasure radiating from her nipple.

Clumsily, he yanked and fumbled with the clasp of her bra until it fell completely free. He shoved it aside and focused on unbuttoning her pants, his mouth never leaving her breast.

He lifted her hips. She hoisted herself up, giving him room to pull her pants down. They fell to the floor and he took a step back and ran his gaze up and down her body.

She felt beautiful and desirable. Even irresistible. He ate her with his eyes. Appreciation didn't adequately describe what she saw in his gaze. This was a man who saw only her. There were no other women.

"I can't say I ever fantasized about having sex with a woman on top of a dresser, but I'm re-evaluating. I can see the appeal."

She wiggled a little closer to him so that she was perched on the edge. Right now she wanted him so much, even the short distance to the bed seemed too much.

He tucked his finger underneath the lace of her panties and ran it along the edge until he delved into her hot, liquid heat. She leaned back, closed her eyes and moaned as he grew bolder with his exploration.

The sensation of his hands rasping lightly over her behind as he cupped her and began to slide her underwear off was enough to drive her beyond endurance. She had to have him. Her nerve endings were fried.

And then she was naked under his seeking gaze and inquisitive fingers. He stroked and caressed until she was a mass of gasping, breathless anticipation.

"No fair," she panted. "You still have clothes on."

He gave her a faint smile before quickly shedding his clothing. Then he dropped to his knees in front of the dresser. His hands slid sensuously up her legs, setting fire with the barest of touches.

Her breath caught and held when he parted her thighs and pressed his mouth to her most intimate flesh.

"Oh…"

It was all she could manage. Everything went fuzzy around her. Swimming. She was swimming in the most exquisite, mind-numbing waters she'd ever navigated.

The man was talented. He was generous. Even when he was pushed to his limits, he brought her to the brink of ecstasy before satisfying his own needs.

"Evan, please!"

He rose up, gripped her knees and yanked her forward until she perched precariously on the edge of the dresser again. There was savage menace in his expression, the look of a man pushed too far too fast and struggling to hold on with everything he had.

He paused only long enough to roll on a condom and then he found her center and plunged deep.

His hands slid under her bottom, gripped tight and pulled her to meet his thrusts. He was deep and she felt him in every part of her soul. She ended, he began. He was a part of her, taking, giving and sharing.

He leaned forward to bury his face in her neck as he rocked against her. Lightning sizzled down her spine as he nuzzled her sensitive skin and suckled the column of her neck.

She wrapped her arms and legs around him until there wasn't an inch of space between them. Still buried tightly inside her, he lifted her up and backed toward the bed. He fell, her on top, and they landed with a jolt.

"Ride me," he said in a strained voice.

His pupils dilated and his brow constricted. Tight lines were etched into his forehead, and his hands gripped her hips so tightly that she could do nothing more than squeeze her inner muscles around his erection.

"Sweat heaven," he groaned.

She wasn't going to last, and she was helpless to do anything about it. She needed to move. She had to move.

Placing her palms flat on his chest, she wiggled free of his grasp and began to move up and down, taking him, releasing him, then taking him again.

Sweat beaded his brow. His eyes were narrow slits, and he never took his gaze from hers. He urged her closer so he could cup her breasts. They filled both palms and he rubbed the pad of his thumb over the painfully erect nubs.

"I can't hold on," she whispered.

"Then let's go together," he urged.

His hands left her breasts and he gripped her hips, lifting her and pulling her down in time with his upward thrusts. The burn spread. Tension mounted. She wound tighter and tighter until it was all she could do to hang on.

She threw her head back, her mouth open in an endless cry of agony. The sweetest, most breathtaking agony of her life.

His hands left her hips to tangle in her hair. He rose up, pulling her harshly to meet his kiss. Frantically, his hands moved up and down her back, into her hair, through her hair, over her face as if he couldn't get enough and wanted to memorize every feature.

And then it was as if the world went silent. The wave rolled, crashed and then broke into a million tiny ripples, each feeding the other.

She was no longer cognizant of holding on to him. She was riding high and fast.

She had no idea how long she lay sprawled over Evan, her heart beating so frantically that she literally felt each thud. His arms were wrapped around her, and their legs were all tangled up. He was still buried inside her, and she could feel the remnants of his orgasm. Each little pulse sent a tiny shock of aftermath flooding through her body.

Slowly she became aware that he was stroking her back and her hair. He murmured little sweet words in her ear but nothing seemed to make sense. She was completely befuddled by this man, by her reaction to him.

"I think I blew it again."

She smiled and snuggled a little closer, tucking her head under his chin and nuzzling his chest.

"You blew, all right. But I think I blew first."

His chest heaved as he chuckled. "You're such a naughty girl."

Summoning energy she sorely lacked, she raised her head and propped up on his chest so she could stare down into his eyes. What she saw sent a pang of longing straight through her heart.

He looked content. Sated, but not just in a sexual way. He looked at home, like they'd been together forever. Oh, she had an overactive imagination. She was sure of that. But when he looked at her like that, with the world in his eyes, a world where only she existed, it was hard not to get caught up in the fantasy they'd created between them.

He ran a gentle finger over her mouth. "What are you thinking?"

"I'm fairly certain a man should never ask a woman what she's thinking right after sex," she said lightly.

"I'm fairly certain all women like to talk after sex. Well, talk and cuddle, or some girly thing like that."

She grinned and leaned down to kiss him. "I like the cuddle part."

He gathered her in his arms and rolled until they lay on their sides. "Not a talker, huh?"

She reached down and carefully rolled the condom off him. He put his hand down to stop her.

"No, I'll do that. You don't have to mess with it."

But she already had it off. She kissed him again then scooted off the bed to discard it. When she looked back, he was propped on one hand, watching her intently.

His naked body was a gorgeous sight. Even in a relaxed state, his proportions were generous to say the least.

"If you keep looking at me like that, it's not going to stay down," he growled.

"You only have one condom?" she asked in mock horror.

He reached over, grabbed her arm and yanked her back down beside him. "I'll have you know, I had a case delivered."

She snorted with laughter. "A case? Are you planning an orgy?"

"I may have exaggerated…slightly. But only slightly," he said with a sly grin.

"That's good to know. I'd hate to think I was under that kind of pressure."

He tweaked her nose then followed up with a kiss. "Somehow I think you could hold up quite well."

She cuddled deeper into his embrace. She hadn't lied about the cuddling part or the talking part. Well, maybe about the talking part. In truth, she'd love to bare her soul, learn all his secrets, tell him all hers. Tell him how much she loved…

She froze. For a moment she simply couldn't breathe. It wasn't as if she'd just fallen in love with the man. No, it had probably been coming for a while now. But she hadn't admitted it. Hadn't even thought it much less said it aloud.

Yeah, it was there in the background just waiting for the time when she let it slip in. She'd been so good—or so she thought—about keeping her emotional distance.

She loved this man. Her heart seized. It was a painful admission. Wasn't figuring out you were in love supposed to be accompanied by fireworks, a fanfare, a giddy thrill? Wasn't it supposed to be the most wonderful thing in the world?

Why then did she have the sudden urge to run to the bathroom and throw up?

"We have options," Evan said.

She blinked and focused her attention back on the here and now and the fact she was in bed after hot, sweaty sex with the man she…loved.

It was all she could do not to groan.

"What options?" she asked huskily.

"I can feed you. I can make mad, passionate love to you again. Or we can take a short nap and then do either option one or two. Or both. See? I'm easy."

She smiled and squeezed him. She did love him. It scared her to death just how much she loved him, and now that she'd admitted it, she was flooded by so much emotion. It was all she could do not to blurt it out like some teenage girl with her first crush.

"Am I staying over?" she asked. She hadn't wanted to assume, but she needed to know before she started choosing options.

He leaned up and cradled her so he looked down at her. "Of course. That is, if you want to. If you didn't bring clothes to go to work in, I can have my driver take you home."

She swallowed. "I did bring clothes. But if he takes me to work, I'm without a car. It would probably be best if he did take me home early enough for me to get my car. I can dress here."

He looked for a moment like he'd say something but then evidently he thought better of it and didn't push. She wondered what he'd wanted to say, but like him, she didn't push.

"All right. I'll make sure we get an early enough wake-up call for you to shower and get ready here before he takes you home to get your car."

Unable to resist, she kissed him. It wasn't a playful little peck this time, but a warm, deep kiss that showed without words the depth of her feelings.

When she finally drew away, his eyes were glazed with passion, but there was also contentment that she didn't want to speculate about.

"In that case, I vote we go with eat, mad passionate love and then sleep," she murmured.

"Sold."

A half hour later, they sat cross-legged on the bed, devouring the room service Evan had ordered. She was swallowed up by one of his robes, and he was wearing a pair of boxer shorts.

She ate indelicately, with her fingers, foregoing the

utensils. It was finger food anyway, and it was too scrumptious to be all highbrow about eating it.

They were nearly done when it hit her that she still hadn't broached the subject of the baseball game. Where before she'd felt a little awkward about bringing it up during what was obviously an illicit rendezvous, here with Evan, she was completely at ease.

"Tell me your plans for the rest of the week. Are you returning to Seattle until our presentation on Friday?"

He cocked his head and studied her intently. "That depends, I suppose."

"On what?"

"On whether I have a reason to stay."

Her cheeks warmed. His meaning couldn't have been more clear. Her mouth suddenly went dry and she gulped a mouthful of water.

"I meant to invite you to the Tide season opener. I have tickets. Good tickets. Are you interested?"

He looked a little surprised, and for a moment she wondered if she'd overstepped her boundries. But then he smiled. A genuine, warm smile that told her he was pleased with her invitation.

"I'd love to go. It's Thursday night, isn't it?"

She nodded. "I could pick you up and drive us over."

His eyes gleamed, and for a moment she could swear he looked victorious. Over what, she hadn't a clue.

"Just tell me what time, and I'll be waiting with bells on."

"It starts at seven, so I'll be here around five-thirty."

"I'm looking forward to it already."

She relaxed. Things were shaping up perfectly. She'd take him to the game and introduce him to Noah afterward. Then she'd wow him the next morning with a kick-ass presentation. The deal was hers. In the bag. She couldn't contemplate any other outcome.

Golden Gate and Athos Koteas might be coming on strong, but they didn't have Noah Hart, and they damn sure didn't have her ideas. Ideas she knew were perfect for Evan and his company.

This was hers.

Evan reached out to wipe a smudge from the corner of her mouth. She glanced down to see his food gone and most of hers, as well. And the way he was looking at her, she had a good idea what was for dessert.

"Give me two seconds to clear this away and roll the cart out into the hall and we'll get on with option two, although I'm thinking that option three should be significantly delayed."

She raised an eyebrow and her heart started tripping double time.

"Oh? How delayed?"

"Very delayed," he said silkily. "I'm thinking option two could be divided into options three, four, five…"

In response, she untied her robe and tugged it away until she sat naked on the bed.

Fifteen

Celia pulled into one of the reserved parking spaces at the stadium and cut the engine. She glanced over at Evan. "Ready?"

He looked out the windshield at the proximity of their space and the stadium entrance and whistled in appreciation.

"These must be some tickets you have."

She smiled. "I told you they're good."

They got out and Celia led the way. Normally she would have gone in through the players' entrance, but she didn't want to tip her hand just yet, so they headed through the main gate just as everyone else did.

Evan waited for her while she went through security and had her bag screened and then they had their tickets scanned and walked in the direction of the field.

Since she'd handled the tickets, she knew he hadn't seen them and she couldn't wait to get his reaction to the behind the home plate VIP tickets she'd scored from Noah.

Several minutes later, and after navigating two entrances, they entered the field above the home plate. She flashed her tickets and an usher led them down the steps to a box of seats directly behind the batter's box.

He motioned them into the row and Celia settled in the seat four rows up from the bottom.

"Wow," Ethan said as he took his seat beside her. "I mean, wow. How the hell did you get these tickets? They must have cost a fortune. Not to mention they've been sold out. I know because I've tried to get them."

"I know people," she said smugly.

He eyed her curiously. "I'm beginning to get the impression you do."

They caught the tail end of batting practice and then settled back as the field was watered and prepared for the start of the game.

Evan relaxed in his seat and knocked his shades down over his eyes. It was exceptionally sunny today and there was absolutely no cloud or fog cover. It was a perfect day for baseball.

In typical business-geek style, his gaze roved over the fans, looking for those who wore Reese designs. If Celia had her way, a lot more normal, everyday people would want to wear his line of sportswear.

He turned when he heard Celia talking to a hot dog vendor. She twisted to look at Evan. "You want something?"

"Whatever you're having," he replied.

He dug into his wallet to pay the vendor, but the older man smiled and waved him off.

"Our Cece is taken care of. No charge for her."

Evan watched the banter between Celia and the vendor in utter bemusement. They chattered about batting averages, who to watch in the coming season and the travesty that had occurred the previous season when the Tide had finished one game back from the division leader.

"They'll win the pennant this year," Celia consoled. "Noah is in top form. He was only warming up his bat last year."

The vendor nodded enthusiastically. "I believe you're right, Miss Cece. He got hot and the season ended."

Celia turned and made an expression like she'd forgotten something.

"Oh, my manners are horrible. Please forgive me. Evan,

this is Henry Dockett. He's worked here since the stadium was built thirty years ago. He knows everything there is to know about everything around here. Henry, this is Evan Reese."

Evan extended his hand to shake the older man's and Henry's face lit up.

"You're the Evan Reese from Reese Enterprises?"

Evan smiled. "One and the same."

Henry nodded approvingly. "Good place for you to be then. Miss Cece will show you a good time."

Someone else signaled for Henry and he nodded at Evan and Celia. "I'll be back later on to check on you, Miss Cece."

She smiled and patted Henry on the arm and thanked him for the hot dogs.

When she turned back in her seat, Evan leaned over to take his hot dog from her lap.

"Do you have everyone eating out of your hand, *Miss Cece?*"

She actually blushed and ducked her head.

"Henry is an old friend."

Evan chuckled, delighted at the rosy bloom of her cheeks.

"Do you have any other surprises in store for me today?"

"Maybe," she mumbled around a bite of hot dog.

The Tide took the field, and the very first batter walked. Celia groaned her dismay along with the rest of the crowd.

"Our pitching has been what's let us down in the past," she whispered to Evan.

He didn't have the heart to tell her that not only did he know, but he could quote the stats for every one of the Tide's pitching roster.

"This year should be better," Evan consoled.

She nodded. "Soren is our best. He usually starts cold, though. If we can get out of the first inning, he's awesome."

Again Evan grinned and sat back to watch. Celia bolted from her seat when the second batter grounded to second and Noah scooped, tossed to the shortstop who turned the double play to first.

Evan could swear that Noah looked straight at Celia and winked. He looked between the two and finally shook off the absurd notion.

Soren struck out the next batter and the Tide was up to bat. Celia clutched her hands like an anxious mother. Todd Cameron, the lead off, looked up at Celia as he headed to the plate, grinned and waved. Celia waved and blew him a kiss.

Evan stared but didn't say anything. Things just got stranger and stranger. He was willing to put the first off as a fluke, but when the third batter came up and gave Celia a thumbs-up, he wondered what the hell he was missing.

After the batter flied out to center field, advancing the two runners on a sacrifice, Evan leaned over, intending to ask Celia exactly what he was missing out on, but she put her hand on his arm and squeezed hard.

"Just a minute. Noah's up!"

Her fingers dug into his arm like little daggers, but he didn't pry her away. He was too interested to see what would happen when Hart came up. And, too, he was interested to get a close up glimpse of what he hoped would be his company's golden PR boy.

Noah's face was drawn in concentration as he began the walk to the plate. He swung the bat a few times then stopped, two inches out of the box. He turned and glanced first to the right of Evan and Celia and dipped his head in acknowledgment. Then he turned and scanned behind home plate until his gaze lighted on Celia.

He lost the look of intense concentration, and his face

relaxed into a smile. He gave her an exaggerated wink and then held up his fist.

Evan's mouth fell open as he glanced between the two. Celia's hand tightened further on his arm when Noah took the first strike.

"Come on, come on," she whispered.

The next two were balls. Then he swung at the second strike. If he didn't hit soon, Evan was going to lose the feeling in his arm.

The next pitch, Noah fouled back. The next was a ball, making it a full count.

"I can't watch," Celia whispered.

The pitcher wound up, threw a fastball and Noah swung. The bat connected with a sweet crack that to anyone listening signaled a smash hit. The ball sailed over the center-field wall into the upper deck. Three-run homer to start the game.

Celia lunged to her feet and screamed at the top of her lungs. "Did you see?" she yelled at Evan. "Did you see?"

"I saw, I saw!"

He laughed as she continued to bounce up and down. Noah rounded the bases, taking high fives from the first- and third-base coaches. He met his teammates at the plate, where the group jumped up and down and pounded on Noah.

Noah looked up at Celia and pointed. She leaped to her feet again and pointed back, her smile so wide Evan was sure she'd hurt something.

Then she glanced over in the direction that Noah had first looked when he'd come up to the plate and then back down at Evan.

"I'll be right back, okay? I'll just be a second."

She hurried up the row of seats and then cut over to the section that adjoined the home-plate area. Evan watched as she hugged two younger looking men and an older guy.

They glanced over in Evan's direction once but then didn't look back as they chatted with Celia.

A few minutes later, she returned and took her seat beside Evan again. He was beginning to think he'd been dropped in an alternate reality. Was there anyone here she didn't know?

When she'd offered Noah to him on a virtual silver platter, he'd only assumed that she'd contacted him through his agent and offered him a deal he couldn't refuse. He hadn't considered that she had such a connection to his team. And what connection that was had Evan insanely curious.

He leaned over so she'd hear over the still insanely celebrating crowd. "What am I missing here?"

She smiled. "I'll explain later. Just enjoy the game."

Mysterious little wench. He'd make her pay later when he had her alone.

The rest of the game followed a similar pattern. Celia seemed to know every damn person on the team. He began to have uncomfortable thoughts, like whether or not Celia was involved with Noah Hart. It would certainly explain how she'd been able to get him to agree to the endorsement deal.

But it also brought up a lot of questions. Like whether she was using Evan to further her career. He glanced sideways at her. No way. It would take someone pretty diabolical to have a man like Noah Hart on the line and then sleep with Evan to secure his business. Why would she even need it if she was involved with Hart? The man made a lot of money, even without the million-dollar endorsement deals. He was one of the highest-paid baseball players in the league.

Before he could get carried away with thoughts that would only enrage him, he made himself back down and quit speculating. He'd find out before the end of the day.

One way or another. And then he'd decide what to do about Celia. And his account.

When the game ended after the visiting team failed to score the necessary runs to overtake the Tide in the ninth inning, Celia stood, her cheeks flush with excitement.

"We're going to have an awesome season. I just know it!"

He stood beside her unsure of what would happen now. Nothing had gone the way he'd anticipated.

Sure enough, she grabbed his hand and began pulling him toward the exit. "Come on," she said.

But they didn't leave the stadium. Instead they went down to a restricted area, where Celia flashed a pass he hadn't seen up to this point. He shouldn't be surprised. But when they stopped outside the players' locker room, he was.

They waited a good while. Several members of the press came and went. Finally one of the players stuck his head out the door, looked up and down and then his eyes brightened when he saw Celia. Evan was a little starstruck. It was the Tide's catcher, Chris Davies. He was a veritable legend in baseball, and it was rumored this would be his last year before he retired.

"Cece! You should have just come on in. Noah got held up by an interview, but he wanted you to come on back."

Celia walked over and gave the catcher a big hug and a kiss on the cheek. "Good game, Chris. You're looking as awesome as ever."

The big man actually blushed. He glanced up at Evan, and Evan was convinced the guy scowled at him.

"Oh, Chris, this is Evan Reese. Evan, this is Chris Davies, the Tide's star catcher."

"Yes, I'm well aware," Evan said. "Great game. I've watched you a lot of years."

"You Evan Reese who makes the sportswear?" Chris asked.

Evan nodded.

"Cool. You two come on back. Noah should be done by now."

Despite his wealth and position, Evan couldn't control the incredible rush of walking into the Tide's locker room. It was every little boy's dream. It was why he'd gone into the business he had. He loved sports, and he was as in awe of the big dream as any other kid out there who loved sports.

Several players stopped Celia for a quick hug and a kiss. Some ruffled her hair and she gave them affectionate pats in return.

"Cece! There you are."

Evan looked up to see Noah barreling his way through a crowd of people. The next thing he knew, he had Celia in a giant bear hug, swinging her around in a circle.

Evan watched, his irritation growing more with each passing second.

Finally Noah put her down.

"Hey, did you see? Fantastic hit, wasn't it?"

Celia smiled broadly at the other man and her affection for him was obvious. A fact that made Evan even grumpier. Endorsement or not, he was ready to deck the star right in the jaw.

"I saw, of course. You were awesome as always."

"Hey, I need to get a quick shower. You two can wait for me over there," he said, gesturing toward a sitting area that was removed from the chaos of the open locker room. "I won't be long."

Celia kissed his cheek. "We'll be there. Take your time."

Noah ruffled her hair affectionately and loped off toward the showers.

Evan opened his mouth to ask but then shook his head. He'd wait. This had to be worth the price of admission.

Celia led him into the adjoining room and sat on one of the leather couches.

"This is usually reserved for coaches and their families," she said when he sat down in one of the chairs across from her. "None of the press or players will come in here."

"You know I have a hundred questions, *Cece,*" he said drily.

She flushed a little guiltily. "Okay, so maybe I'm guilty of wanting to watch you experience everything firsthand. I mean I could have warned you but that wouldn't have been any fun."

He raised an eyebrow. "The only question I want answered right now is whether you're involved with Noah Hart."

He watched her eyes go wide in shock. Her mouth fell open, and he knew in that moment, whatever he might have assumed—even with good reason—he was dead wrong.

"It was a sensible assumption," he defended before she could speak.

"Evan, Noah is my—"

They were interrupted when the three men Celia had gone to visit in the stands came through the door.

"Cece, love," the older man said when his gaze lighted on her. He smiled big and held out his arms. Celia went into his embrace and endured a painful-looking bear hug.

The other two men regarded Evan with what could only be considered as suspicion.

"Going to introduce us, Cece?" the bigger man asked.

"Of course," she said as she curled her arm around the older man's.

"Evan, I want you to meet my family. This is my father, Carl, and these two are my brothers, Adam and Dalton.

Guys, this is Evan Reese. He owns Reese Enterprises. I brought him back to talk to Noah."

Evan could swear she said the last pointedly. He relaxed and shook the hands of each man and endured a painful grip from each. Typical measuring stick of a man. See if you could make the other wince. He squeezed back with as much force and endured grudging looks of respect from her family.

Interesting that they were all back in the players area and that they'd sat in different areas for the game, although Celia had said she'd gotten the tickets particularly for him.

"Very glad to meet you, sir," he directed at Celia's father.

"Are you the man responsible for my Cece working so many long hours?"

Evan lifted one eyebrow then glanced between Celia and her father. Celia closed her eyes in despair and shook her head helplessly at Evan. He remembered her saying that according to her father and brothers, her only requirement was to look pretty and let them support her. Apparently they weren't on board with her having a career.

"I'm afraid I am, sir. I wish I could say it was something I regret, but Celia is one of the brightest minds I've encountered. She's going to single handedly turn my advertising efforts around. I think in a year or two, Reese Enterprises won't simply be one of the leaders in athletic apparel, but the *undisputed* leader when it comes to sportswear.

Her two brothers eyed Celia with renewed interested while Celia stared at Evan, her eyes wide with shock. He could almost swear she looked a little teary. He smiled at her and reached for her hand. To his surprise she accepted without complaint and curled her fingers tight around his.

"If you're meeting Noah about business, we'll just scoot on out," her father said. "You going to make Sunday dinner this time or will you be busy again?"

"No, I'll make it," she said as she leaned up on tiptoe to kiss his cheek. "Sorry about last weekend. Something came up."

Evan realized that he was what came up when he'd finessed Celia away for the weekend. While he was sorry she'd missed what was evidently an important family gathering, he couldn't summon any regret for the way their weekend in Catalina had come together.

"It was nice meeting you all," Evan said sincerely.

The other men nodded and shook his hand again before departing the room.

"Interesting family," he said when they'd gone.

Celia sighed. "I love them dearly, but they're pretty insufferable."

"It's obvious they love you a lot."

She smiled. "Yeah, and I love them to pieces, too. Warts and all."

A moment later, Noah Hart ambled into the room and once again gave Celia a bone-crushing hug. Then he turned to Evan and looked back at Celia.

"So, is this the man?"

"I'd say you're the man if you agree to front my new line of athletic wear," Evan said, taking charge of the meeting.

"Evan, I'd like to you to meet my brother. Noah Hart," Celia said as she stepped forward. "Noah, this is Evan Reese, owner of Reese Enterprises."

Evan eyed them skeptically. Her brother? Everything made a hell of lot more sense with that revelation. And what was with the different last name? To his knowledge, Celia hadn't married, or was this one more thing she'd kept him in the dark over?

His question must have been obvious even to Noah, because he grinned and slung an arm over Celia's shoulder.

"Cece had a different father—well, different mother, too. Kind of a long story but my father married Celia's mother when Cece was just a baby. We helped raise her, especially when her mom died when Cece was so young. Hence the reason her last name is Taylor."

Evan cleared his throat. Here he'd been granted a once-in-a-lifetime opportunity, and he was more concerned with finding out Celia's secrets than securing a deal with Noah Hart.

"I thought it might be best if you and Evan went to dinner and talked about the deal Evan is offering," Celia inserted.

"What about you?" Evan asked sharply. He hadn't counted on Celia leaving him and Noah. Hell, he hadn't even realized he'd be meeting Noah so soon. Suddenly his plans for a night of making love to Celia didn't seem so realistic.

"I have other plans," she said lightly. "Besides, I really have nothing to do with this part. You and Noah need to discuss the possibilities. I'd just be in the way."

Noah shrugged then looked at Evan. "You like barbeque?"

"Love it."

"Good. I know this great place just a few blocks from here. We can grab dinner and talk."

"I drove him here, Noah, so you'll need to give him a ride back to his place. That okay?" Celia asked. She turned to Evan. "I'll see you tomorrow morning. Nine o'clock at the Maddox."

"I can have my driver meet me," Evan said. "It's not a problem." He glared at Celia as he said it. The woman was ditching him. What he'd thought was finally an effort to see him outside of a business setting had, in fact, just been a business meeting in disguise. He'd deal with her later, though. Right now he had a sports superstar to woo, and he'd be damned if he let his irritation with Celia interfere.

Sixteen

Celia paced the Maddox conference room. Her nerves were wound tight, and she'd meticulously gone over every little detail of her presentation. The televisions out front had mock-ups created by the media folks. An endless stream of Reese Enterprise promotion ran on the video monitors and the art department had framed several print-ad options and displayed them in the conference room.

With fifteen minutes to go time, the other members of her team had assembled. Tension was high but so was excitement. Ash had congratulated her on landing the biggest client for Maddox thus far, but he'd acted distracted and distant. Celia wondered if he was indeed having issues with the rumored girlfriend.

The others had all been quick to add their congratulations. No contract had been signed, but they all seemed convinced that after this morning, Reese Enterprises would be in the bag. She hoped they were right.

Noah had called last night after an extended dinner with Evan. Apparently after barbeque the two had gone for beers and spent the evening like old college buddies.

Evan had extended an extremely cushy offer, one that had surprised even a very jaded Noah. The two were meeting later with their respective lawyers to iron out the details, but Noah said he'd agreed.

"Okay, we've got five minutes," Celia said. "Let's take our places and get ready to knock his socks off."

They took their seats along the conference table. Brock

smiled at Celia and gave her a thumbs-up before taking a seat next to Elle. Jason took the seat next to Ash, who frowned and reached into his pocket for his phone.

"Excuse me for a minute," he said as he rose from his seat. He crossed the room out of earshot to take a phone call.

The intercom buzzed and Shelby announced that Evan had arrived. "Shall I show him back?" she asked.

Celia took a deep breath, looked at her coworkers lining the conference table all ready to do their part, and said, "Show him back, Shelby."

As Celia ended the conversation, Ash returned to the table.

"Sorry, but I have to go," he announced. "And I'm not sure when I'll be back. Hopefully no more than a few days. I'll let you know when I have more details."

He turned and strode out of the room, leaving Celia and the others to stare after him in astonishment. Celia glanced over at Brock and raised an eyebrow. Brock shrugged and gestured for her to continue on. Whatever was up with Ash would have to wait. This meeting was too important to all of them.

Seconds after Ash's abrupt departure, Evan entered behind Shelby. Celia crossed the room and extended a hand to Evan. Instead of shaking it as she'd intended, he slid his fingers over her palm and held it far too long for her liking. She snatched it away and turned to introduce him down the row.

Her presentation went off without a hitch. Each part of her team executed their part flawlessly, and through it all, Brock sat back with a very satisfied expression on his face.

By the time she was done, she was as convinced as everyone else that Evan would sign with Maddox. He'd be a fool not to.

The lights went back up after her last video clip.

"This concludes our presentation," she said to Evan. "I hope we've convinced you of our commitment to you and your company."

He took his time responding. For a moment he studied her, his hands in a V in front of him. Then he simply nodded.

"I'm very impressed. My question is, how soon can we move on this?"

Rosa was packed with the after-work crowd, but the entire back room was filled with Maddox employees, all celebrating their biggest coup to date—Reese Enterprises.

Celia was high on her achievement, but she couldn't shake the anxiety over her relationship with Evan. She'd avoided him last night when she'd all but dumped him on Noah. She'd avoided him after her presentation when he'd wanted to take her to lunch to celebrate.

Brock passed out champagne to everyone then called for a toast. He saluted Celia with his glass and the room erupted into cheers.

She smiled her pleasure, but all she could think was that she'd rather be with Evan. And that was a very big problem.

"For a girl who's the toast of Madcom, you don't look very happy."

Celia turned to see Elle standing beside her, drink in hand. She tried to smile but then gave up with a sigh. "Am I that obvious?"

Elle shrugged. "Probably not. I doubt others are paying too much attention to you. You looked…distracted."

"I'm in a mess, Elle," Celia admitted. "I don't know what to do."

Elle wrapped a comforting arm around her. "Surely it can't be that bad?"

"I'm involved with Evan Reese. Intimately."

Elle stiffened. "Oh. Maybe you're right."

Celia couldn't help but notice the way Elle's gaze drifted to Brock, who stood across the room talking with Jason Reagart. Brock turned and caught Elle's gaze, and what Celia saw there made her pause. Possession.

"I didn't intend for it to happen," Celia said. "I know better. Me of all people should know better. I've kept it secret, and it's driving me insane. I worry over who'll see us together and whether they'll draw the wrong conclusion. I'm so tired of sneaking around. The worst part is I'm in love with him."

Elle made a sound of sympathy and pulled Celia away from the others until they stood in a dark corner.

"You need to be honest and open about this, Celia. If you don't, it'll tear you apart," Elle said earnestly.

Elle was so sincere and her words were so heartfelt that Celia wondered if she was speaking from personal experience. Was it possible that Elle was having a secret fling with Brock? If the looks between the two were any clue, there was some serious chemistry there.

It was on the tip of her tongue to ask, but she didn't want to hurt Elle, especially if she didn't want anyone to know.

Instead she squeezed Elle's hand. "Thank you, Elle. I know you're right. I just have to figure out how to handle this. It's giving me a headache."

"First thing you should do is enjoy your moment in the sun," Elle returned. "This is your night to shine. You worked hard for this, Celia. Go have some fun."

"Okay, okay, Mom," Celia teased. "I'm up for another drink if you are."

Elle smiled and the two women headed for the bar for another round. Celia endured another series of toasts, backslaps and loudly yelled congratulations. Elle was right. This was her night. It was the culmination of weeks of hard work and long hours. Damn if she wouldn't enjoy every minute of it.

* * *

Celia's cab pulled up to her apartment, and she pulled out several bills to pay the driver. While she was far from toasted, she hadn't wanted to chance driving home, so she'd left her Beamer at work and taken a cab from Rosa.

It was late, but not ungodly so, and she was still riding high from the celebration.

The cab pulled away and across the street she saw Evan leaning against his car, watching her. He started forward, and she stood there like a statue, watching him approach.

"Out celebrating?" Evan asked with a slight smile.

She nodded. "After-work thing. Took a cab back so I didn't have to drive."

"You should have called me. I would have had my driver take you home."

"I don't think that would have looked good if the man whose account I just landed sent a car to take me home after my celebration party."

He regarded her with no expression. Then he asked, "Going to invite me in?"

As if she'd tell him no.

He fell into step beside her as they walked to her door. He waited while she unlocked the door and then followed her inside. As soon as she locked up behind them, he had her in his arms.

Not again. She couldn't lose all control of her senses the moment he touched her. It wasn't normal.

"Do you have any idea how turned on I was watching you take control of that presentation this morning?" he said between kisses. "You were glowing and you were such a hardass. I wanted so bad to drag you into a closet and have wild, crazy sex."

He always knew exactly what to say to melt any resistance on her part. He was a seducer with words.

He had her clothes off before they got to her bedroom.

How he knew where it was, she didn't know. Maybe all men had a natural instinct for where to find the nearest bed.

They went hard and fast. No matter what their intentions, that first time was always desperate, like it was their last. She gripped him, he cradled her, she kissed him, he thrust into her.

It was crazy, irrational, it was the most erotic, bone-melting sex of her life.

And she loved him beyond all reason and sanity.

She lay under him, holding him close as he panted against her neck. She was positively weak, and thank God they were on the bed, because she wasn't moving. It wasn't possible.

Finally Evan rolled away and threw his arm across the bed with a groan.

"Every time, I swear, I'm going to take it slow, make love to you with all the finesse I'm capable of. Then I see you and the teenage hormones start revving out of control, and I become some seventeen-year-old on steroids."

Celia died laughing and then moaned when she moved too much. "I would have liked a seventeen-year-old on steroids with your sexual know-how when I was seventeen. All the boys I knew thought a kiss and quick grope was all the foreplay necessary before penetration."

"I'd say what morons they are if I hadn't just practically done the same thing to you," he said in a pained voice.

She rolled into the crook of his arm and laid her head on his chest.

"You don't hear me complaining, do you? I haven't thrown you out for being an inconsiderate toad."

He kissed the top of her head. "And for that I'm extremely grateful."

She snuggled into his arms. "Are you going back to Seattle for the weekend?"

He went still and then tightened his arm around her. His hand lay possessively on her hip.

"There's no reason we can't go public with our relationship now, Celia. It's all over. You have the account."

She sucked in her breath.

"But, yes, I do need to go back to Seattle and tie up some things. I plan to spend a lot more time in San Francisco over the next few months and I need to make arrangements."

Her heart sped up. Did he mean he was staying in San Francisco to be near her? She hated guessing, but she hated assuming even more.

She was still uneasy about the timing of them seeing each other. It was too close to when he'd signed on with Maddox.

"I'll be back Monday afternoon. I want to spend the evening with you. Dinner. Dancing. You can stay over at the hotel and my driver will take you into work on Tuesday."

She loved it when he got all demanding. She was a sucker for someone who planned in detail, and he'd certainly planned their evening down to her staying over for what would undeniably be amazing sex.

"When do you leave?" she asked quietly.

"First thing in the morning."

She leaned up on her elbow so she could look him in the face. "Then what are you doing here?"

He rolled her into his arms and under him again. "I can sleep on the short flight home."

She made a show of checking her nonexistent watch. "You have six hours left. What do you plan to do with them?"

"I'm going to show you just how good I am at time management," he murmured as he swept down and hungrily devoured her lips.

Seventeen

After a Sunday of fielding curious questions from her brothers about Evan, Celia was relieved to go into work on Monday. She wasn't ready to admit to even her family that she and Evan were anything more than business associates. They knew what had happened in New York and that it was complete nonsense. She loved them for their undying loyalty and their absolute faith in her. Which was why she was reluctant to confess to a relationship with Evan. It would only muddy the waters even though she and Evan both knew the truth.

She was late, thanks to a traffic snarl that lasted an entire hour and an already late start from her apartment. By the time she made it off the elevator, it was closing in on noon, and her mood was in the toilet.

When she saw Shelby, she knew something was wrong. The usually cheerful receptionist eyed Celia with something that looked suspiciously like pity, and she refused to hold Celia's gaze for long.

Not even wanting to know what that was all about, Celia bypassed her usual meet and greet with Shelby and headed for the sanctuary of her office. To her surprise, Elle was waiting for her.

"Hello, Elle," Celia said as she came in and tossed her briefcase onto her desk.

Elle's face was drawn, and she looked like she was dreading talking to Celia. In her hands was a folded newspaper or magazine. Celia couldn't tell.

"Celia, there's something you need to see. Everyone else has already read it. I tried to call you but couldn't reach you at home or on your cell."

Celia's stomach sank. She didn't like the look on Elle's face or the way she was coming at her with that paper.

Elle plopped the newspaper on Celia's desk and it was then that Celia saw it was a gossip rag. Her nose wrinkled in disgust.

"Elle, what are you doing reading that crap?"

"Look at it, Celia."

Elle jabbed her finger at the photo spread and the headline. Celia looked down and all the blood drained from her face. She had to grip the edge of the desk to keep her knees from giving way.

There were pictures of her and Evan at Mitchell's wedding. The same pictures she'd received via e-mail from Evan's mother. One was of them dancing and her laughing up at him. The other was of Evan kissing her. Her hand was splayed over his chest and there was no mistaking the huge rock on her third finger.

The headline blurred in front of her, but she got the gist. It was all about Evan and his new fiancée and was it coincidence that Evan had allegedly signed a contract with Maddox Communications, the agency where his fiancée worked.

She scanned the article, but she was too furious to continue past the insinuation that Celia had spent the last several weeks doing whatever was necessary to land Evan's business.

"That's not all," Elle said grimly.

She walked around Celia's desk and jostled the mouse so that her screen came up. She typed in a URL and navigated to an advertising community site that hosted a blog and a message board, mostly used by advertising professionals. There in the latest blog post was the picture of

Evan kissing her along with the announcement of Evan going with Maddox Communications. The subtitle was short and to the point, and made no bones about the way they thought Celia landed the account.

Celia sank into her chair, stunned. Absolutely and completely stunned by what she'd read.

"My God, Elle, what do I do?" she whispered.

Elle squeezed her shoulder in sympathy, but her eyes told Celia she was at as big a loss as Celia was as to how to handle it.

"Does everyone in the office know?" Celia asked painfully. "Have they all seen it? And what do they think?"

"Well, Ash hasn't been back in, so I don't know if he's seen it. I know Brock and Jason saw it because I was in Brock's office with both of them. Jason didn't have much to say but Brock was pissed."

"At me?"

Elle shook her head. "I don't know, to be honest. I doubt it. He's not the type to get angry before he hears your side. Besides, you got the account. It shouldn't matter to him how you did it."

"That's true, I guess. It only matters to *me*."

"I'm sorry, Celia. Really sorry."

Celia put her hands over her face. "I was stupid, Elle. I was stupid, and now I have to pay the price."

The sound of someone clearing their throat had Celia looking up toward the door. Brock stood there, an indecipherable expression on his face.

"Elle," he said. "Would you leave me and Celia for a moment?"

"Of course," Elle murmured as she hurried away.

Tears burned Celia's eyes. She was holding on by a sheer thread.

"Want to talk?" Brock asked.

It was that question that did it for Celia. If he'd been

angry or if he'd been indifferent, she could have handled it, but the simply worded request broke her down.

Her shoulders shook, and she lowered her head as a sob welled from her throat. It appalled her that she'd cry in front of her boss. But there was no holding back the release of the crushing pressure that had been building over the course of the last few weeks.

Brock didn't say or do anything. He just stood there while she gathered herself together again. When she looked up, he sat in one of the chairs in front of her desk and waited for her to speak.

"It's not how it looks," she said as she wiped tears from her cheeks.

He glanced at the spread out paper on her desk. "Well, it looks like you were wearing his ring, but you're not now."

With a sigh, she explained the whole sorry tale about her trip to Catalina with Evan and how she hadn't felt like she could refuse when he was short on time and ready to move on his campaign.

She left out the mushy details she'd shared with Elle. Brock was, after all, A. her boss and B. a man. He didn't need to know that she'd stupidly fallen in love with a man she'd be working with for a long time to come. It made things entirely too messy. What if they broke up? Would Evan feel weird about continuing the relationship with Maddox or would he take his business elsewhere?

There were a million reasons why she should have never ever gotten involved with Evan, and yet, she hadn't heeded any of the warning signs.

"I overheard what Elle said about how it shouldn't matter to me how you got the account. I won't lie. It doesn't. Furthermore, it's none of my business unless you broke the law or did something to damage the reputation of Maddox. I don't think this qualifies. My concern is for you. I know how devastated you were by what happened in New York.

"I meant what I said when I told you that you had my support. That hasn't changed. I'll make sure to put an end to any speculation going on in the office, but I can't control what people think or say outside the work area. I don't imagine this is going to be easy for you to deal with in the next little while, but Maddox Communications stands behind you."

"Thank you, Brock," she said in a shaky voice. "That means a lot to me."

"Any idea who would have done this?" Brock asked.

She frowned and stared down at the pictures. Then she looked back up at Brock.

"These pictures were on my company computer. Evan's mom sent them here. They've only been here. I don't imagine Evan's ex has any love for me, but she and Mitchell left immediately on their honeymoon. They haven't even seen the photos yet. So other than me, and maybe Evan if his mom showed them to him, the only other person who's seen them is his mom. These weren't taken by the professional photographer. Evan's mom shot these with her digital camera, and I don't believe for a minute she'd go to these lengths to discredit me. She was too damn excited over our supposed engagement."

Brock swore long and hard. "Are you sure this is the only place you had them?"

Celia stared back at him. "You don't think…surely not. No one here would do something like that."

"I don't know, but I'll find out," he snapped.

He rose and stalked to the door. Then he paused and turned back for a moment. "Don't let this get you down, Celia. I have a feeling that whoever did this intended just that. You did a damn good job on this account. No one can take that away from you unless you let them."

Then he was gone, leaving Celia sitting there like a deflated balloon.

She was supposed to meet Evan in just a few hours. Their evening was already planned, complete with the sleepover at his hotel and his driver taking her to work in the morning. She'd already had reservations about it all, but now the idea made the knot in her stomach grow even larger.

Who the hell had released those pictures? It made her furious. Why would anyone even care or go to such lengths to discredit her?

She wouldn't put it past Athos Koteas. He'd made it a point to tar Maddox Communications any way possible, but how would he have gotten his hands on those pictures?

The idea that one of her coworkers was responsible made her want to puke. She couldn't believe it and work here another minute. She had to push that possibility out of her mind or go insane.

How sick was it that she didn't even want to venture out of her office now? She couldn't face everyone knowing that they'd seen that damn article.

She laid her head on her desk and tried to ignore the painful ache that had developed around her temples.

She knew what she had to do, and it hurt far more than those damn pictures. But she hadn't worked this hard to rebuild her reputation and her career to have it go down the toilet over one torrid affair.

The rest of the day was spent sequestered in her office. She only spoke to Shelby to tell her she wasn't accepting any calls and the rest of the time she spent in brooding silence.

At five, she stared out the window, watching as her coworkers left the building. She purposely waited until everyone else had left before she locked up her office for the night.

Though it was well past seven, she dragged herself down six flights of stairs just on the off chance any stragglers were in the elevator. She was pathetic and spineless but she didn't care. She'd face them all when she had some semblance of control over her emotions.

She drove to her apartment with her fingers curled tightly around the wheel. She battled bouts of fury and the impulse to break down into tears. By the time she reached home, she was mentally exhausted.

To make matters worse, Evan was waiting for her by the door. He wore a deep frown, and his brow was creased with concern.

"Where the hell have you been?" he demanded. "I was worried. We were supposed to meet here an hour and a half ago."

She couldn't even meet his gaze as she jammed her key into the lock. She shoved the door open, and went inside, allowing the dark to swallow her up.

"Hey, Celia, what's wrong?"

He flipped on the light, and she winced. He was in front of her immediately. He grasped her arm and tilted her chin up with his other hand.

"What the hell? Have you been crying?"

She closed her eyes and tried to pull away, but he held tight.

"Talk to me, dammit."

"We can't see each other for a while," she blurted out. "Okay? We need to cool it. Things are crazy. My life is crazy."

Her words did what she hadn't been able to do. He let go of her arm and took a step back.

"Want to run that by me again? In a way that I understand?"

There was a wary look in his eye that warned her this wouldn't be easy. But then he didn't give a damn about what people thought. He wasn't ruled by the opinions of others. As she had so many times before, she wished she could be like him.

Instead of answering him, she rummaged in her bag for the stupid gossip rag and then she thrust it at him as if it was self-explanatory. And it was in a way.

He glanced over the paper and then looked back up at her. "So? What's the problem?"

She knew he'd react that way. Positively knew it, and it drove her crazy. She wanted to scream and rail at him, but she'd come across as some hysterical banshee, and then he'd never take her concerns seriously.

"That's not all," she said stiffly. "It's all over the Internet. An advertising community site has it on their blog along with some snotty little line about how I got the account after the announcement of you signing with Maddox."

He looked blankly at her. "I fail to see what the big deal is, and I damn sure don't see why it's any cause for us not to see each other anymore."

She gritted her teeth. "You fail to see. Well, I don't, Evan. This is my career we're talking about. My reputation. Which I might add is in shreds now. Everyone in my office saw that. Everyone in the advertising community saw it. Everyone knows, or thinks they know, just how I got you to sign with Maddox. It doesn't matter if it's true. It's what everyone thinks. Our announcement of our agreement will be posted in *Advertising Media*. Right on the heels of those pictures. Do you know how that looks?"

She stopped and swallowed back the damning sob that welled up in her throat.

"How am I supposed to go out on my next client call? What if the client is male and what if he expects the same favors I granted you? Or maybe he'll agree to sign with Maddox if I sleep with him."

"I'll kick his ass," Evan growled.

"You can't be there to kick everyone's ass, Evan. That's what I'm trying to tell you. The best thing you can do for me is to back off until the smoke clears."

He blinked and then his eyes went cold and hard. "Is that what you want, Celia? What you really want?"

She was afraid to answer, afraid to confirm after that terrible look that had come over him. But she wouldn't lie.

"Yes," she whispered.

His lip curled in derision. "I won't be anyone's dirty little secret, Celia. I'm tired of running around like two people having an affair behind their spouses' backs. I made the mistake of settling once. I'll never do it again."

"Evan, please, it's not like that. I just need some time," she pleaded.

"It is like that, Celia. It's very much like that. It's apparent to me that I'm definitely not first on your list of priorities. Or even second or third. There's a hell of a lot of things that rank higher than me. I don't give a damn who knows that we're sleeping together. And I damn sure won't continue to sleep with someone who does."

He turned and stalked toward the door. He flung it open and caught it with one hand, turning as he stepped out.

"If you change your mind, don't bother to come crawling back. I think you've made it abundantly clear what I'm good for."

The door slammed, and Celia's heart shattered into tiny little pieces. She stared numbly, hoping, expecting that he'd come back and tell her they could work things out, that he'd wait.

Minutes passed, and the sickening realization hit her that he wasn't coming back. Not only had she lost her reputation, and possibly her career, but she'd lost the one man she loved enough to have risked it all in the first place.

Eighteen

Tuesday morning, Celia took the coward's way out and called Brock to schedule vacation time for the rest of the week. He didn't like that she was hiding. It was no way to face the issue, but after hearing how horrible she sounded, he didn't argue the matter further.

The rest of the day she spent moping around her apartment, alternating between anger and fits of upset.

Wednesday, she packed a bag and headed for the one place she knew she could lick her wounds in safety. Her dad's house.

He took one look at her and held out his arms for a giant bear hug. She needed it. Never had the comfort of home felt so good to her than now.

He sat her down and cooked her a huge breakfast, because in his book, there wasn't anything that couldn't be cured by a big, home-cooked breakfast.

All the time she ate, he sat beside her, eating his own food in silence. He didn't pry or demand answers. It was what she loved most about him. He never intruded into his children's lives. No, he didn't have to. He just waited for them to come to him, and then he'd move heaven and earth to make everything right again.

Only this time he couldn't fix it.

She spent the afternoon on the couch, watching television with him. He babied her endlessly, fixing her a snack in the afternoon and even baking her favorite cookies. Chocolate chip with no nuts.

By the time evening rolled around, it was obvious her father had spent the afternoon on the phone with her brothers. They arrived, one at a time, and made it a point to shower her with lots of hugs and endless pampering. Or at least Adam and Dalton did.

When Noah showed up, he took one look at her and demanded to know what the hell had happened. She burst into tears which prompted Adam, Dalton and her dad to threaten to dismember him for upsetting her.

"Well hell, Dad, I didn't upset her. It's obvious that someone did, but it sure as hell wasn't me!" Noah protested. "Hasn't anyone asked her what's wrong yet?"

"We were waiting," her father said gruffly.

"Waiting for what?" Noah asked in exasperation. "For her to cry?"

Celia wiped at her eyes and tried to stop the sniffling. She knew her brothers hated it when she cried. Especially Noah.

Noah turned to her, his eyes softening at the signs of her distress. Then he sat down on the couch next to her.

"This doesn't have anything to do with Evan Reese, does it?"

Despite her vow to cease and desist, his question spurred another round of tears.

"Good going, bonehead," Adam growled.

"Anyone ever tell you that your skill with the opposite sex sucks?" Dalton asked.

Noah put an arm around her and squeezed comfortingly. "What happened, Cece?"

"Oh God, Noah, it was awful. The paper printed these horrible pictures and this blog said horrible things. My career is shot to hell. My reputation is in shambles and Evan doesn't want to see me anymore because I asked him to back off until the smoke cleared. He thinks I think he's my dirty little secret, and he hates it. And me."

She dug her palms into her eyes and rubbed until it felt like she was scraping her eyelids across sandpaper every time she blinked.

"Whoa," Adam said. "Did any of that make sense to the rest of you?"

Dalton and her father exchanged helpless looks.

Noah sighed. "Maybe you should back up and start with what the newspaper printed and what the blog said and why your career and reputation have been dragged through the mud."

"It's a long story," she muttered.

"We've got all night," Dalton offered.

She sighed and once again poured out the whole story from start to finish, not leaving a single detail out. Except for the sex. Her brothers had a hard time seeing their baby sister as anything other than their baby sister, and telling them about her sex life would only make them turn a sick shade of green. And then they'd probably go after Evan with one of Noah's baseball bats.

"That's crazy," Adam huffed.

Dalton nodded his agreement. Noah, who was a lot more tuned in to just what bad press could do to a career and reputation, was a lot more subdued. Concern flared in his eyes when she got to the explanation of the article and blog.

"That sucks," Noah said.

Celia nodded. "Tell me about it."

"So where does this Evan person fit in?" her dad asked. "I mean, there seems to be a big piece missing here. You were pretending to be his fiancée and this paper prints stuff about you, and you said he's angry because he thinks you think he's your dirty little secret. Am I missing something?"

She sighed. "I'm in love with him, Dad. And now he hates me."

All four men's mouths rounded into Os.

There was marked silence, and she regretted having blurted out that fact. Love was girly stuff, and none of the men looked like they had a clue what to say or do next.

"Look, I appreciate you guys. I love you all to pieces. I don't know what I would do without you. I don't expect you to fix this for me. I'm thirty years old. Not a little girl anymore. The days of me coming to you with my scrapes and boo-boos should be well behind me. I'll figure out something. I just needed a place to lick my wounds and regroup."

Adam frowned. "Now, you wait just one damn minute. You're family, Cece. I don't care how old you are."

Even Dalton scowled and nodded his agreement. Noah merely squeezed her hand and told her bluntly to shut up.

"You'll always be my little girl and their little sister," her dad said in his soft, gravelly voice. "That don't change because you go away to college, get a fancy degree and get a job that beats you down every chance it gets."

She winced at the direction this was heading.

"We love you and we'll always be here for you to come running to. You got that?"

"Yeah, Dad, I do."

"Now come here and give your old man a hug. Sounds like you've had one hell of a week."

She scrambled up from the couch and threw herself into his beefy embrace. She squeezed for all she was worth and inhaled his scent.

"Love you, Dad," she muffled out against his shirt.

"I love you, too, Cece. Don't you forget it, either. Now back up and tell me more about this Evan fellow and if I need to round up your brothers to go beat him up."

Evan's office staff was avoiding him. Not that he could blame them. He'd arrived back on Tuesday, acting like a bear with a sore paw. He'd briefly touched base with his assistant, long enough to tell her not to hurry back in to work and to remain with her granddaughter as long as she was needed.

He'd gone over his last conversation with Celia until it rolled like video footage through his head. No matter how hard he tried, he couldn't get it to turn off.

It was his own fault for pursuing Celia so relentlessly. She'd been hesitant from the start, and he'd ignored all the warning signs. He'd never become serious about a woman who didn't put him first. And he damn sure wouldn't be involved with a woman who put more importance on what the world around her thought about her than on her relationship with him.

He scowled when a knock sounded at his door. One of the secretaries poked her head in and held up an envelope like a shield.

"This just came for you, sir."

"Bring it over," he said, waving her in.

She hurried over and all but threw the envelope at him before beating a hasty retreat out of his office. He shook his head. He hadn't been that bad since he'd returned two days ago.

Okay maybe he had.

With a sigh, he glanced at the envelope. It was an overnight package with the name of some corporation from San Francisco he'd never heard of before. It was marked extremely urgent.

He opened it and to his surprise it only held a folded newspaper. Nothing else. No letter, no explanation. He pulled it out and it fell open on his desk. It was turned to a specific page, and when he looked down, he saw Celia's picture, only it wasn't one he was familiar with. She looked different. Maybe younger? And she looked terrified in the picture. She had one hand up like she was trying to avoid the camera.

Frowning, he scanned the article. He was so pissed by the time he got to the end that he had to go back and read it more carefully.

The photo was indeed of a younger Celia when she lived and worked in New York. She'd landed a position with a prestigious advertising firm one year out of college. She'd done impressive work and then she'd been promoted to senior executive—above several other junior executives who'd been there longer.

A relationship with the CEO had been quickly revealed, and Celia had been named in the divorce proceedings between the CEO and his wife. Celia had fled New York in disgrace to return home to San Francisco, where she took a job with the smaller, on-the-rise Maddox Communications.

Only last week, intimate photographs of Celia Taylor with billionaire Evan Reese had appeared in another article the day after Reese had reportedly signed a multimillion-dollar advertising contract with Maddox.

Blah, blah, it went on and on, vilifying Celia and along with her, Maddox Communications. His stomach churned, and he felt the urge to go vomit.

His gaze caught the latest issue of *Advertising Media*. Fresh off the press and delivered just this morning. It was just as Celia had said. The announcement was there for the world to see, but it was tainted by those photos.

He picked up the paper and stared at it again. There was no way. No way in hell she'd done what they accused her of. He hadn't known Celia for long, but he damn well knew she wouldn't have done something like this. If she did have a relationship with this bastard, it wasn't so she'd get a promotion.

He wanted to go kill someone. Preferably whoever had started this smear campaign. No one messed with the woman he loved and got away with it.

All the air left his lungs in a painful jolt.

Loved?

He liked Celia. Liked her a damn lot. She was beautiful, vibrant, sexy as hell. She was a great lover and partner. He had fun with her. He loved her company. But did he love her?

The knot in his stomach grew. How could he be so stupid about his own personal life? Surely it would have occurred to him before now if he was in love with someone.

He stopped and let his thoughts catch up with the breathless, panicky feeling in his chest.

How had he gone thirty-eight years with never having fallen in love? He'd never even contemplated the idea until now. He wasn't at all sure he liked it, either.

Love was such a messy emotion. It was bound to be inconvenient. You sure couldn't put it on a schedule and love never played by the rules. He liked rules. And schedules.

Ah, hell, he was absolutely in love with her.

It was why he was sitting here in such a terrible mood that his usually easygoing office staff wouldn't come near him for fear of being decapitated.

He looked again at the article, and his chest utterly caved in. Celia. God, he'd been such an idiot. A complete and utter, madly-in-love moron.

He'd reacted just like a petulant child, furious that his favorite toy was being taken away. In this case, Celia had wanted to put their relationship on hold and all he could see was that she was pushing him away. He'd panicked. He'd been a total ass.

She needed him. Needed his support. And he'd told her to take a hike. Worse, he'd arrogantly told her not to bother changing her mind and come crawling back.

He winced. Holy hell in a bucket but he'd said some horrible things. If there was any crawling to do, it would be him doing it. In the mud. Over broken glass.

Her tear-stained face came painfully to mind. The hell

she must have endured. Her coworkers had seen the photos. Everyone in her profession had likely seen them. They'd all probably come to some very inaccurate conclusions.

He'd been selfish and demanding from the start. He hadn't given one moment's consideration to how their relationship would reflect on her. It had all been about him. His wants and needs. He didn't care if anyone knew about them, but she had. And with good reason.

He should have been standing with her. He should have supported her. Now it looked as if the world had turned on her, and where was he? Off licking his wounds while she faced the world alone.

To hell with that.

He had a woman to win back.

Nineteen

Celia sipped her hot chocolate and stared over her dad's backyard to the ocean in the distance. She'd always loved the view here. His house was perched on a cliff, though it was situated a good distance from the drop-off.

As a child, after reading about mudslides, she'd been convinced that they'd fall into the ocean. Her brothers had told her it was far more likely they'd fall off in an earthquake. She shook her head at the memory of how they liked to torment her.

It was peaceful here, and not for the first time, she wondered why she'd been so anxious to move away. True, her family could be overbearing at times, but they loved her. They were loyal and they'd do anything in the world for her. That wasn't something to run away from. It was something to hold on to and never let go.

No, she wouldn't leave again. She was through discovering the world. Her world was here. Home. Where her family lived.

The sliding-glass doors opened and Noah stepped out. She turned all the way around in her chair to greet him, but stopped when she saw the expression on his face.

"I was about to say good morning," she said as he came over and plopped down beside her.

He sighed and held out another newspaper. "I thought about not showing you this, but I knew if something was being said about me, I'd want to know about it so I wouldn't be blindsided."

Dread began low in her stomach. She stared fearfully at the extended paper. Then her disgust overcame her apprehension and she plucked it from his hand.

There in black and white for the entire Bay area to see was a detailed account of all that had happened in New York. Oh, it was a *blatant* smear campaign. It was written in the guise of an article announcing the deal brokered between Reese Enterprises and Maddox Communications.

It detailed her job history, colorful as it was, to the present and hinted broadly about there being a relationship between her and Evan.

Nothing was left to the imagination. Everything she'd worked so hard to overcome had been splashed in excruciating detail.

She should be angry. Furious even. But what she felt was…resignation.

She looked up into the worried eyes of her brother as the realization hit her.

It would always be something. Evan was right to be angry that she'd placed more importance on what others thought of her than she did on what *he* thought of her.

As long as the people she loved knew the truth, it shouldn't matter what some stranger thought. Brock believed in her and her abilities. She had the backing of her agency. Her family loved her unconditionally. Evan evidently didn't care who knew they were involved, so why should she?

For the first time in a long while, she looked at her life with a sense of deep gratitude. For so long she'd been shaped by external forces. Her desire to shed the protective grasp of her family. Her need to escape from the scandal in New York and prove herself to everyone around her.

The only person she'd been proving anything to was herself. Everyone else had known all along what kind of person she was.

"Oh, Noah, I've been so stupid," she whispered.

He cocked his head in confusion. She responded by throwing her arms around his neck and hugging him fiercely. Then she drew away and kissed him on the cheek.

"Thank you."

He still looked supremely puzzled. "For what?"

"For opening my eyes. I've been so very blind to what was in front of me all along."

He grinned crookedly. "Well, okay. Do me a favor and the next time Adam and Dalton start riding my ass, you remind them that I opened your eyes. Whatever that means."

She smiled back. "What it means is that I'm through trying to please others. I'm through caring what they think about me. The only people in this world who matter to me already believe the best of me. What more do I need?"

"Don't let these bastards get you down, Cece. You're right. We love you to pieces and nothing anyone ever insinuates is going to change that. Furthermore, I know good and damn well that the girl I helped raise isn't a manipulative, calculating bitch who doesn't care who she hurts on her way up the corporate ladder."

She hugged him again. "Thank you, Noah. You have no idea what that means to me."

He leaned away, still holding her arms. "So what about Evan?"

She pressed her lips together. "He told me not to bother crawling back if I changed my mind. Well, too bad. I made a mistake. It's not the end of the world. We all make them. I'm sure he's made his share. He was angry and I'm sure he didn't mean half of what he said. I'm going to make him listen to me. Then I'm going to take the leap and tell him I love him and hope like hell that doesn't make him run for cover."

Noah touched her cheek in a tender gesture. "If he

does, he's a fool who doesn't deserve you. Remember that, okay?"

She glanced down at her rumpled appearance. She shuddered to think what her hair looked like. She's spent the last three days moping.

"I need to go jump in the shower and then I have some apologizing to do in person."

Noah got up, leaned over and kissed her on the forehead. "Good luck."

He held his hand out to help her up. She hurried inside, determined not to waste another minute without telling Evan she was sorry and that she loved him.

She took a while in the shower mainly because she was working out just what she wanted to say to Evan. Simple vanity also made her want to look her absolute best. I mean, who went and groveled when they looked like a hag with a hangover?

She pulled on a robe and twisted a towel around her hair. Then she walked through her bedroom and into the hall on her way to the kitchen. She needed something to eat, and she needed to tell her dad she'd be leaving in the next hour.

When she rounded the corner into the living room, she looked up and nearly fell over in shock. There, sitting on her father's couch, was Evan. Noah and her father were nowhere to be found.

"Oh, no," she whispered. "No, no, no." This wasn't supposed to be the way she confronted him.

She turned, intending to make a mad dash for her bedroom and shut the door until she could make herself presentable. He caught her before she'd gone three steps.

He grabbed her arm and pulled her into his arms. "No, Celia, don't go. Please."

She moaned in frustration. "Dammit, Evan. You've ruined everything. I was going to look nice when I came to apologize. Now I'm in my bathrobe and my hair is all wet and in a towel. I don't even have any makeup on."

Then it hit her. What was he doing here? At her dad's? How had he even known where to find her and, moreover, why would he care?

He chuckled and pulled her even closer. "I don't give a damn what you look like. I need to talk to you. Personally I don't think you've ever looked better to me."

She narrowed her eyes at him. "What are you doing here, Evan? How did you know where to find me? I was about to leave to go find you."

"Then it's good we found each other," he said softly.

He tugged her back into the living room. "Come sit with me, Celia. Please. There's so much I need to say to you."

"Ditto," she murmured.

She let him pull her down beside him on the couch, even if she was still horrified by the fact she was wearing a robe, with nothing on underneath, and she was wearing a wet towel on her head, for God's sake.

But when she looked at him, she promptly forgot all that. All she knew was that she loved this man, and she'd do anything to make things right between them.

"I'm sorry," she said in a low, shaky voice.

He pressed a finger to her lips. "Shh. I don't want to hear that word cross your lips. It's me who is sorry. I was an ass. I said despicable things to you."

Her eyes widened, and she felt the ridiculous urge to cry again, as if she hadn't done enough of that in the last few days.

"First, I want to talk about this," he said as he drew out the dreaded newspaper clipping from his pocket.

She froze, her stomach seizing with dread.

"Don't look like that. I don't believe a word of it. But it's obviously an important part of your past. It hurt you and it's affected a good portion of our relationship. I want you to tell me what really happened."

Her lips trembled and she twisted her hands nervously in her lap. "I got out of college, intending to rule the world. I moved to New York. I loved it there. Such a big, busy city, and I was away from home, away from my family. At the time that was important to me. I was stupid."

"I think we all go through the desperate need to get away from our family," Evan said.

She shrugged. "So there I was, out to take on the world. I landed a job with a prestigious agency and I worked my butt off to advance as rapidly as possible. I was good and I knew it. So when I got promoted, it wasn't a surprise to me. There were people who'd been there longer who were pissed, but I knew I deserved it. I felt like I deserved it.

"And then one day my boss called me in his office to congratulate me, and he let me know at the same time what he expected in return for the favor he'd granted me."

"Son of a bitch," Evan growled.

"I was horrified. And a bit naive because I honestly hadn't seen it coming. I didn't even know what to do at first, other than turn him down flat. I was stupid enough to think that would be the end of it."

Evan scowled and reached over to take her hand.

"I buried myself in work, convinced that if I worked harder, landed more accounts, that he'd just go away. One night I was working late and he dropped in to see how I was doing."

She made a derisive sound deep in her throat. The memory strangled her. She hated that helpless feeling.

"He came onto me hard and didn't intend to take no for an answer. He probably would have raped me if his wife hadn't burst in. I think she knew what was going on, but she didn't care. She had her way out of the marriage and a way to make him pay for everything he'd ever done wrong to her in their marriage.

"I was named the other woman. Everyone knew what happened. I had no defense. Suddenly I was a woman who'd slept her way to the top and then destroyed my boss's marriage. Believe me when I say no one was lining up to do business with me. So I quit and came home. Brock gave me a shot with his agency and the rest, as they say, is history."

Evan closed his eyes and let out a sound of disgust. "I was so unfair to you, Celia. You tried to tell me so many times how our relationship might affect you and your career, but I wouldn't listen. I was selfish and egotistical. I was determined that I should be enough for you. What a jerk I was. I wasn't even here when all hell broke loose. I should have been beside you, shouting to the world that you were my woman and I was damned proud of it. Instead I slunk off like a sulking two-year-old when I didn't get my way, and I can only imagine how it looked."

He gathered both her hands in his and brought one to his lips. He kissed each finger. "I'm so sorry. I hope you'll let me make it up to you. I wish you would have told me all this sooner. Maybe I would have understood you better. But I also know I gave you no reason to trust me. That's going to change. I want you in my life. I'll do whatever it takes to make that happen."

She stared at him in utter bewilderment. "What are you saying?"

"I'm saying I love you. That I'm sorry. That I want another chance and that it's me who's crawling back on hands and knees, begging for your forgiveness. You'll never lack for my support again, Celia. You'll always have me to lean on. And I'll personally throttle anyone who so much as whispers an ill word about you."

Her throat closed in. Her mouth went dry. The world tilted a little crazily around her.

"But I was going to you to apologize," she whispered. "I was wrong, Evan. I did put too much importance on what others thought. As long as I have the support of those who love and respect me, it doesn't matter what the rest of the world thinks. I should have to crawl back. I was *horrible* to you."

"No, no, my love," he said as he hugged her tighter to him. "Never crawl. *Never.* Forget I said it, please. You weren't horrible. You were upset. Your world had been upended, and I should have been the one person you could come to and who would support you and understand. I didn't even try to understand. I got angry and stormed away. I love you. Please forgive me."

"Oh, Evan, I love you, too. So much. I do forgive you as long as you'll forgive me, too."

His entire face lit up. He looked almost boyish as he stared at her in wonder. "You love me? You're not just saying it?"

She smiled and kissed him. She wrapped her arms around his neck and put every ounce of her love into her kiss. He lifted her up until their mouths were even and their noses bumped.

"How did you find me?" she asked.

Evan sobered and he let her slide back down until her feet touched the floor. He cast her a sheepish look. "I might have stormed into Maddox Communications, threatening death and destruction if someone didn't tell me where the hell you were. I'd already tried your apartment, your cell phone. I even called Noah's agent because I couldn't reach Noah, either."

Celia giggled. "Death and destruction? Noah's agent?"

"Well, maybe not death and destruction but I did threaten to pull my contract if I didn't get some answers.

Let's just say that the entire Maddox team developed a sudden interest in your whereabouts. Someone found Adam's business number, had him paged and then waited an eternity for him to call back. He told us you were here and I came right over."

She shook her head, but her grin was so big she couldn't hide it.

"Did you mean it?" he asked softly. "Do you love me? Enough to put up with my ogre ways and my demanding personality? Enough to marry me?"

She sucked in her breath as tears flooded her eyes.

"I think I can tolerate you," she said teasingly. "If you can tolerate the fact that I can't cook worth a darn. I'll probably never meet you at the door wearing an apron, and the thought of having children scares the bejesus out of me."

A slow grin spread across his face. "I think I can handle all that. So will you? Marry me? Put me out of my misery?"

"You don't mind me keeping my job? I've fought too hard and have spent too long coming to grips with my issues regarding public opinion. There's no way I'd want to quit now."

He cupped her chin and smoothed a thumb over her cheek. "You can't quit. You're handling all my advertising. I'd be broke inside of a year without you. Besides, I'm way too damned proud of you to ever want to clip your wings."

"I love you," she said fiercely. "And, yes, I'll marry you."

He lowered his head to hers and kissed her long and sweet. "I love you, too," he whispered.

He reached down into his pocket and pulled out the same ring he'd given her before. He grasped her hand in his and slid it back on her finger.

"I've kept this in my pocket ever since you gave it back.

I can't tell you how wrong it felt when you handed it back to me that night. Promise me you'll never take it off again."

She glanced down at the glittery diamond, tears blurring her vision. Then she glanced back up at the man staring at her with so much love in his eyes that her knees threatened to buckle.

"Never. This time our engagement is for real."

* * * * *

If you love Maya Banks,
look for

THE MISTRESS
THE BRIDE
THE AFFAIR

Available now as ebooks,
only from Harlequin!

And for more sensual and passionate reads
from Harlequin Desire, try

COURTING THE COWBOY BOSS
by USA TODAY bestselling author
Janice Maynard

and

ONE WEEK WITH THE BEST MAN
by Andrea Laurence

Both available November 2015!

REQUEST YOUR FREE BOOKS!
2 FREE NOVELS PLUS 2 FREE GIFTS!

H HARLEQUIN®

Desire

ALWAYS POWERFUL, PASSIONATE AND PROVOCATIVE

YES! Please send me 2 FREE Harlequin® Desire novels and my 2 FREE gifts (gifts are worth about $10). After receiving them, if I don't wish to receive any more books, I can return the shipping statement marked "cancel." If I don't cancel, I will receive 6 brand-new novels every month and be billed just $4.55 per book in the U.S. or $5.24 per book in Canada. That's a savings of at least 13% off the cover price! It's quite a bargain! Shipping and handling is just 50¢ per book in the U.S. and 75¢ per book in Canada.* I understand that accepting the 2 free books and gifts places me under no obligation to buy anything. I can always return a shipment and cancel at any time. Even if I never buy another book, the two free books and gifts are mine to keep forever.

225/326 HDN GH2P

Name	(PLEASE PRINT)	
Address		Apt. #
City	State/Prov.	Zip/Postal Code

Signature (if under 18, a parent or guardian must sign)

Mail to the **Reader Service:**
IN U.S.A.: P.O. Box 1867, Buffalo, NY 14240-1867
IN CANADA: P.O. Box 609, Fort Erie, Ontario L2A 5X3

**Want to try two free books from another line?
Call 1-800-873-8635 or visit www.ReaderService.com.**

* Terms and prices subject to change without notice. Prices do not include applicable taxes. Sales tax applicable in N.Y. Canadian residents will be charged applicable taxes. Offer not valid in Quebec. This offer is limited to one order per household. Not valid for current subscribers to Harlequin Desire books. All orders subject to credit approval. Credit or debit balances in a customer's account(s) may be offset by any other outstanding balance owed by or to the customer. Please allow 4 to 6 weeks for delivery. Offer available while quantities last.

Your Privacy—The Reader Service is committed to protecting your privacy. Our Privacy Policy is available online at www.ReaderService.com or upon request from the Reader Service.

We make a portion of our mailing list available to reputable third parties that offer products we believe may interest you. If you prefer that we not exchange your name with third parties, or if you wish to clarify or modify your communication preferences, please visit us at www.ReaderService.com/consumerchoice or write to us at Reader Service Preference Service, P.O. Box 9062, Buffalo, NY 14240-9062. Include your complete name and address.

HDI5

SPECIAL EXCERPT FROM

HARLEQUIN

Desire

*When Bailey Westmoreland follows loner Walker Quinn
to his Alaskan ranch to apologize for doing him wrong,
she can't help but stay to nurse the exasperating man's
wounds, putting both their hearts at risk…*

Read on for a sneak peek at
BREAKING BAILEY'S RULES,
the latest in New York Times *bestselling author*
Brenda Jackson's
WESTMORELAND series.

Bailey wondered what there was about Walker that was different from any other man. All it took was the feel of his hand on her shoulder… His touch affected her in a way no man's touch had ever affected her before. How did he have the ability to breach her inner being and remind her that she was a woman?

Personal relationships weren't her forte. Most of the guys in these parts were too afraid of her brothers and cousins to even think of crossing the line, so she'd only had one lover in her lifetime. And for her it had been one and done, and executed more out of curiosity than anything else. She certainly hadn't been driven by any type of sexual desire like she felt for Walker.

There was this spike of heat that always rolled in her stomach whenever she was around him, not to mention a warmth that would settle in the area between her legs.

Even now, just being in the same vehicle with him was making her breasts tingle. Was she imagining things or had his face inched a little closer to hers?

Suggesting they go for a late-night ride might not have been a good idea, after all. "I'm not perfect," she finally said softly.

"No one is perfect," he responded huskily.

Bailey drew in a sharp breath when he reached up and rubbed a finger across her cheek. She fought back the slow moan that threatened to slip past her lips. His hand on her shoulder had caused internal havoc, and now his fingers on her face were stirring something to life inside her that she'd never felt before.

She needed to bring an end to this madness. The last thing she wanted was for him to get the wrong idea about the reason she'd brought him here. "I didn't bring you out here for this, Walker," she said. "I don't want you getting the wrong idea."

"Okay, what's the right idea?" he asked, leaning in even closer. "Why did you bring me out here?"

Nervously, she licked her lips. He was still rubbing a finger across her cheek. "To apologize."

He lowered his head and took possession of her mouth.

Don't miss
BREAKING BAILEY'S RULES
by New York Times *bestselling author*
Brenda Jackson, available November 2015 wherever
Harlequin® Desire books and ebooks are sold.

www.Harlequin.com

HDEXP1015

Turn your love of reading into rewards you'll love with

Harlequin My Rewards

**Join for FREE today at
www.HarlequinMyRewards.com**

Earn **FREE BOOKS** of your choice.

Experience **EXCLUSIVE OFFERS** and contests.

Enjoy **BOOK RECOMMENDATIONS**
selected just for you.

PLUS! Sign up now
and get **500** points
right away!

Earn **FREE REWARDS**
HarlequinMyRewards.com
Join Today!

MYR16R